Dear Mom, in Ohio for a Year

Dear Mom, in Ohio for a Year

Cynthia Stowe

SCHOLASTIC
HARDCOVER

Scholastic Inc.
New York

*Thanks to Nola Thacker, editor at Scholastic,
for her invaluable help with the creation
of this book.*

Library of Congress Cataloging-in-Publication Data

Stowe, Cynthia.
    Dear Mom, In Ohio for a Year / Cynthia Stowe.
      p. cm.
    Summary: When she is sent to stay with free-spirited relatives in
rural Vermont while her mother finishes college, Cassie must adjust
to a new school and a very different way of life.

    ISBN 0-590-45060-3

    [1. Country life—Fiction.   2. Schools—Fiction.]   I. Title.
PZ7.S8915De   1992
[Fic]—dc20   91-46545
                                                                CIP
                                                                 AC

12 11 10 9 8 7 6 5 4 3 2 1   2 3 4 5 6 7/9

Printed in the U.S.A.   37

First Scholastic printing, September 1992

To Robert

Chapter One

Cassie hated taking the school bus. She wouldn't tell Aunt Emily or Uncle Fred, but she was afraid: afraid of the clunky bus that bounced her to the ceiling when it went over a bump, afraid of the crowd of faces that watched her, afraid of waiting alone at the end of the driveway.

You couldn't say it was deserted, where Cassie was waiting on that September morning. There was just no one there. No one was supposed to be there, on a mountain road.

Aunt Emily said it wasn't really a mountain. Uncle Fred complained that there was altogether too much building on it, what with the four houses going up last spring. Cassie longed for what she remembered from home, the rows of three-story houses with their neat little lawns.

She missed them in her stomach. It was the worst of what she missed, except for her mother, of course.

The yellow bus came clattering to a stop, and Cassie got on for the third day in a row, staring down at the stairs as she climbed. She was near the end of the school bus route, so there were only a few seats left in the front. Cassie didn't mind. She was glad to slide into a seat in the front with the little kids, turning away from the faces behind her.

The ride took forever. They went down Fox Den Road, and then right and left, and left again on narrow dirt roads with pastures and, sometimes, woods on either side. When they finally turned right onto Route 37, they were almost at Northwood Elementary.

Then they were turning into the small, narrow driveway that looked like it was leading into someone's house. But the road widened quickly, and there was the circular driveway and the parking lot for the teachers.

Nobody spoke to Cassie as she got off the bus and headed into class.

Cassie had been placed in Mrs. Kalish's room. Mrs. Kalish was actually the only sixth-grade teacher, because Northwood was so small there was only one class for every grade. Mrs. Kalish had been very strict those first two days, never smiling, but Cassie noticed that she never actually yelled at anyone, either.

Cassie had hoped to be in Mr. DeLorenzo's class back in her old school, because he was nice and funny and, every year, he took them to the Boston Museum of Science. Cassie had really wanted to go to the museum with her class. There were three sixth grades back in her old school, so Cassie knew she had a one in three chance of being in Mr. De-

Lorenzo's class and getting to go. Now, there was no chance.

A girl with long brown hair pulled back into a ponytail leaned over and said, "My sister had her last year, and she says she never smiled once."

"Who?"

"Mrs. Kalish. And she *reads* to us, can you imagine reading to a sixth-grade class? That's for babies. Everybody says she's been here *forever*."

Cassie tried to look interested, but she didn't know what to say, so she didn't say anything. Mrs. Kalish was organized. She told them exactly what to do, and she didn't let anybody get away with anything. Cassie liked that. She'd had a fifth-grade teacher last year who had wanted to be friends with the class.

It hadn't worked. All year, the kids had been noisy and rude. This year, Cassie wanted a regular teacher, with regular rules. If she couldn't live where she wanted to, with her mom, at least she wanted a decent teacher.

The girl with the ponytail was talking again, "My sister says if you don't do your homework, she keeps you in for recess and, then if you still don't do it, you gotta stay after school. She calls your parents and *everything!*"

Cassie was saved from answering by Mrs. Kalish opening morning meeting. Mrs. Kalish was standing in front, all dressed up in high heels and a flowered cotton print dress, tall and somewhat skinny, standing in the same spot she'd stood the last two days, the spot that started morning meeting. Her hair was brown, but it almost looked gray because it was so thin.

Cassie wasn't sure how she did it, because Mrs. Kalish didn't say anything. But when she stood in that spot, gradually everybody's attention was drawn to her, and they all got up and sat in the circle.

Everything was different here. The desks were in a big square all facing each other, not in rows like Cassie was used to. Every year, Cassie tried to get a middle seat, one away from the noisy kids in back, but far enough from the eyes of the teacher. She'd learned that if she casually walked into school on the first day and slid into a middle seat, the teacher usually let her stay unless, of course, there were assigned seats.

The way the desks were in Mrs. Kalish's class, everybody was in plain sight. Nobody could relax in the back. It was hard for Cassie to do her work, being so noticed.

And for meeting, everybody had to leave their seats and sit on the floor in a circle in front of the desks. The first day of school, when she had worn her favorite denim skirt that was a little too short because she'd grown so much, Cassie had thought she'd *die*, sitting there, not knowing whether to put her legs under her or put them out front.

That morning, in meeting, Mrs. Kalish was telling

them about their first writing assignment. "We're going to start out with a couple of small pieces," she said, "just to get warmed up. We'll start on our big projects pretty soon."

Nobody groaned. Cassie was amazed. In her old school, whenever a teacher mentioned writing, half the class sunk lower in their seats. The other half figured they'd just write something and get it over with. But, a big project? What did that mean? How come the kids were just sitting there, not doing anything?

Mrs. Kalish was still speaking. "Today, let's just do an easy thing. You can do anything you like. You can even write about your summer vacation if you want."

Nathaniel was waving his hands in the air. "Can I write about when I threw up all over my father when we were riding the roller coaster at Rotterson's?" Everybody laughed.

Mrs. Kalish sighed. "Nathaniel, if you're able to write it descriptively, be my guest. Add your feelings, if you can. Write about your feelings."

My feelings are none of your business, Cassie thought, and she went back to her desk, pencil in hand, trying to think of a way out. She stared at the blackboard, and wondered about everyone else in the room busily writing. She started to write a sentence and then crossed it out. Her slight body tightened.

Mrs. Kalish was suddenly at her side. She leaned over and spoke softly so that only Cassie could hear. "Having trouble?" she asked.

Cassie shrugged.

"Well, did something nice happen?"

Unexpectedly, Cassie felt her eyes filling with tears. She looked down.

Mrs. Kalish watched her silently. Then, after a few moments, she touched Cassie lightly on the shoulder and asked, "Would it be easier to write at the table? People do, sometimes." She pointed to the art table at the side of the room.

Cassie nodded, and got up and went over. Mrs. Kalish followed her. "If you're having trouble writing about something that did happen, why don't you write about something that didn't. You can make it up."

"What do you mean?"

"Well, you can do a fun thing, like you can say, 'I didn't get to travel to the moon and I didn't get to ride an elephant in the Bronx Zoo.' "

"I can just make it up?"

"Yes. I'm just trying to see how you write. It doesn't matter what you say. Just tell me a story."

"Will you make me read it to the class?"

"No, of course not, not unless you want to."

As soon as Mrs. Kalish was back at her desk, Cassie wrote:

I didn't go to Egypt and ride on a camel
and I didn't go to the mall and buy $5,000
worth of stuff, and I didn't . . .

She stopped. This seemed even harder.

Everyone else was working, and Mrs. Kalish had told her she wouldn't have to read it to anyone. She pushed her short brown hair away from her forehead and went on. "And my mother didn't really go back to school for a whole year and she didn't really leave me in this hick place with people I don't even know even though they're my aunt and uncle and I don't miss my mother at all and I'm not going to to have to stay here for a whole year in this dumb school with these dumb kids."

Somehow, the tears were back. Cassie looked around to make sure that no one was noticing her, and then she wiped them away. She even got her Kleenex and blew her nose, and then she crossed out the last part of her essay. Then, she erased it, because she thought that maybe Mrs. Kalish would be able to read through the lines.

All of a sudden, Mrs. Kalish was collecting the papers and it was too late to do anything else. Cassie figured that Mrs. Kalish would get mad that she hadn't written very much since she'd erased most of her writing. But Cassie passed her paper in, because she couldn't think of anything else to do.

She got it back after lunch. Mrs. Kalish had

written, "You have a good start here!" on the top.

How come she didn't give me an F? wondered Cassie. How come she didn't write something like, "I expect you to accomplish more work!"?

Cassie's old teachers would have. They would have even underlined it. They would have even spoken to her about it because normally Cassie worked so hard and they wouldn't want to see her slip. Cassie sighed. Mrs. Kalish was certainly different from any teacher she'd ever known.

Cassie took the paper and folded it over and over and stuck it in her pocket. Somehow, during the rest of the afternoon, she wanted it close to her.

That night, before going to sleep, Cassie tried to write a letter to her mother.

> *Dear Mom,*
> *I hate it here. Please come home. Please don't make me stay here. How come you're making me stay here? I hate . . .*

She crumpled it up into a tiny ball and threw it in the trash.

> *Dear Mom,*
> *How are you? I am fine. It rained on Thursday. Today, I . . .*

Dear Mom,

I hate it that you left. When you told me you were leaving, I just wanted you to go away, right then. And I wanted you to never come back. Why don't you stay in your stupid old school. Why don't you . . .

Dear Mom,

How come you dumped me off? How come . . .

Cassie crumpled those up, too, and lay down on her bed and stared at the ceiling. She didn't cry. She didn't want to cry. She could hear Aunt Emily and Uncle Fred talking softly in the kitchen and, after a while, she fell asleep.

Chapter Two

Dearest Cassie,

I love my new place! It's in this lovely old Victorian home, and all I have to do for the rent is cook Mrs. Schneider supper and do the laundry. My room is on the third floor, just like our old place. I walk up this rickety flight of stairs and open the door and . . . voilà . . . there I am, in my palace! It's a big room, so I'm going to put my bed against the west wall, and I've already seen a desk at the Salvation Army that I can put under the big windows. It'll be perfect for studying.

So, how are you? I can't wait to get your first letter. Tell me all about living with Aunt Emily and Uncle Fred and school and everything! I want to know everything about your new adventure.

I'll be home before you know it. I miss you.

Love and kisses and thousands of hugs,
Mom

Cassie brought the dishes in from the kitchen and set the table in the dining room. She made little flowers with the cloth napkins, like Aunt Emily had taught her to, and she placed the macaroni and cheese on the slate trivet in the center of the table.

"Let's eat, I'm starved," Uncle Fred said, carrying a basket of garlic bread into the dining room. His wire-rimmed glasses and his red plaid flannel shirt bounced a little with his walk. He wasn't fat, just solid. He was a mason by trade, and he'd already shown Cassie several of the stone walls and chimneys he'd built, as they'd driven around town.

Uncle Fred had a regular face and regular hair, and there was nothing unusual about his appearance. He often laughed and said if he changed his glasses, he could rob banks in broad daylight and nobody would be able to identify him because he looked like everybody else.

Finally all the food was on the table, and Cassie sat down on what had already become "her" place, the chair by the window.

She wasn't used to the grace they said or, rather, didn't say. "Grace" meant that they sat at the table and held hands and closed their eyes and were quiet. Cassie didn't know what to do, so she just kept wishing it was over. She felt embarrassed, holding Aunt Emily's and Uncle Fred's hands.

"Do you and your mom say grace?" Aunt Emily asked, as she pushed her wild, curly hair away from her face. Aunt Emily looked completely different than Uncle Fred. She was tiny in every way, tiny and delicate, but only in a physical sense. She had beautiful masses of dark brown hair that somehow fitted her frame, even though you'd think she should have short hair because of her tininess. She was pretty and quick, and she dressed in midcalf flowing skirts with wide belts and tailored blouses.

Things matched on Aunt Emily. Even when she was working in the garden and wearing old overalls and big painters shirts and sweatshirts, things matched. Even when she was carrying out the trash, she looked rather glamorous. Cassie wished she could look like Aunt Emily.

Aunt Emily worked in a clinic down in Elton. She was a therapist. "Do you say grace?" she repeated.

"Bless this food to our use, amen," Cassie answered.

Aunt Emily laughed. "That's what we used to say when we were kids. But I like our grace better. You can say whatever you want to God."

Cassie didn't answer. She didn't want to say that she preferred her old grace. It was faster and she knew what to do. She also liked watching *Cheers* reruns during supper like she and her mom used to do, bringing their little black-and-white TV onto a chair in the kitchen. Cassie's mom always insisted on them eating at the table, but that was the only rule.

"So, how was your first week of school?" Uncle Fred asked.

"Okay."

"Did you know that your mom and I went to that school?" Aunt Emily asked.

"You did?" Cassie looked up quickly.

"But I spent a lot of my time in the principal's office, especially after the union."

"The union?"

"I started one, in fifth grade. We called ourselves The United Students of Northwood. All the teachers thought it was cute, until the strike."

"You went on strike?"

"You'd better believe it, Cassie," Uncle Fred said. "Your aunt is not known for her passive personality." He reached over and touched Aunt Emily lightly on her nose.

She laughed. "We struck for equality and justice . . . and no homework. We figured that we spent a good eight hours in school, counting the bus trips. Lots of grown-ups only work eight hours, so why should we have to do more?"

Cassie laughed. "What happened?"

"I have honestly never had so many people so mad at me since. I think it was the picketing during recess that really got them. And the signs. Signs like DOWN WITH MENTAL OPPRESSION and HOMEWORK ROTS YOUR BRAIN."

Cassie laughed again. She thought the last one was pretty good. "Did my mom picket, too?"

"She was too little. She was only in second grade. But I think I embarrassed her, even at that age. I think I've always embarrassed your mom."

"Do you think that's really true, Emily?" Uncle Fred asked.

"Kind of," she answered. "But, c'mon, Cassie, have some macaroni and cheese. Pass your plate and I'll serve you." Aunt Emily piled on a large spoonful. "Want more?"

"No thanks."

"But I thought you liked macaroni and cheese. You mom told us it was your favorite."

"Well, I do, but . . ."

"But what?"

"I like the kind in the box."

"But that stuff's loaded with chemicals. This is made with fresh cheddar cheese."

Cassie took a bite and swallowed fast.

"Do you really like it?"

"Yes, thank you." Cassie was old enough to know when she was supposed to lie.

"Pass me your bowl and I'll serve you some salad," Uncle Fred said.

Cassie sat, watching him. She took another forkful of the macaroni and swallowed it quickly.

"You've got to chew better," Aunt Emily told her. "I read this thing that you're supposed to chew each bite of food at least fifty times."

Cassie felt her jaw tighten. "Fifty times? But it would be all mush."

"It's supposed to be. Our mouths are the first stations of our digestive systems. All the enzymes in our saliva start breaking down the food."

"Maybe Cassie doesn't want to talk about saliva during suppertime, dear," Uncle Fred said.

Cassie was grateful to him for interrupting the saliva discussion, but she watched with despair as he piled at least five funny white things on the top of her salad. She wondered if Aunt Emily was going to make her chew all her food fifty times.

"Have some bread, Cassie," said Aunt Emily.

Cassie reached for some with enthusiasm. This stuff was a little browner than usual, but it still tasted good.

"Part whole wheat," Aunt Emily said. "The store was out of our regular whole wheat today, so this stuff will have to do." She helped herself to some. "I have to start making my own again, but today I just didn't have the time."

Cassie said a silent prayer of thanks. She pushed the funny white things to the side of her salad plate, and ate some lettuce and tomato. Then she got her courage up and took another forkful of macaroni and cheese, turning her head to the side, so that Aunt Emily couldn't see that she didn't chew.

"You don't seem to be much of an eater," Uncle Fred said.

Aunt Emily answered for her. "That's not what h'r mother told us."

Uncle Fred was reaching for more macaroni. "Cassie, you need to put some weight on those bones."

Cassie shrugged. She'd always been a little kid, but, last year, she'd shot up four inches to 5'4", and it had made her skinny. Mom had told her not to worry, that she'd gain back her weight in time.

"We'll fatten you up with good, wholesome food," Aunt Emily said.

What did they think she'd eaten at home? Junk?

"Can I have the garlic bread, please?" Cassie asked.

"Sure. How do you like the artichoke hearts?"

"Um, you mean these things?" Cassie moved the white things around with her fork.

"Yes, haven't you had them before?"

"No."

"You're in for a treat. Try them — they're great."

Cassie moved one around a little. She tried to hide it under a piece of lettuce, but she looked up to see both Aunt Emily and Uncle Fred watching her.

"What's the matter?" Uncle Fred asked.

"Nothing."

"Well then, what?"

"They *look* funny," Cassie said.

There was silence. Cassie sat chewing her garlic bread, and Aunt Emily sat chewing her macaroni, and Uncle Fred chewed the artichoke heart he'd popped into his mouth. Cassie couldn't even taste her garlic bread anymore. It felt like she'd chewed it at least fifty times, maybe even a hundred.

Finally, Aunt Emily said, "She doesn't have to eat her artichoke hearts if she doesn't want to." The way

Aunt Emily said it didn't make Cassie feel any better.

"Let's have some ice cream and then go for a walk," Uncle Fred said. "Cherry chocolate chip!"

"Do you want me to help with the dishes?" Cassie asked.

"No, that's okay," Aunt Emily answered. "I'll do them later."

They went for a walk in the old cow pasture behind the house, watching the lightning bugs that were flashing on that hot September evening. Aunt Emily even went back in the house and got a clean peanut butter jar from the recycling bin, and Cassie captured fifteen of the lightning bugs, making her jar burst with light. That part was fun.

Cassie did, however, go to bed hungry.

Later that night, she was awakened by some music playing softly. The music was classical, the kind Mom used to listen to sometimes after Cassie was in bed. At first, she was scared and thought it was a burglar, but then she remembered that burglars probably don't go around with their tape players on.

Cassie got up and looked out her bedroom window. It was Aunt Emily, dancing in the backyard, waving her arms and doing swirls. It didn't look like she had too many clothes on. Cassie gasped and shook her head and went back to bed. She pulled her blanket way up over her, even over her head.

Chapter Three

Cassie woke slowly. As she lifted her arms they felt heavy, as if there were weights attached to her elbows and wrists. She felt sick, but she couldn't say what hurt.

Something was unsettling, and then she knew what it was. It was too quiet as she lay there that Saturday morning. It was silent in a way that Cassie couldn't hold.

In the city, she woke to the train grumbling in the distance, dogs barking, and the sounds of people. Even if people weren't talking, you still knew they were out there, hiding somewhere behind their curtained windows, hiding in the noises of the city.

When Cassie was lonely in the city, she'd go into her room and put her radio on and open her windows, even in the winter. She was used to the city sounds. She missed the horns blowing and the cars rushing past and the radios from other people's houses. Cassie liked to know there were people nearby.

But up here, you knew there was no one. Once in a while, a car drove up the long, steep mountain, but the house was set back so far in the woods that you could barely hear it, even if you listened.

As Cassie woke more fully that Saturday morning, she started hearing sounds in the silence. The birds were singing now, as if they'd just discovered that Cassie was awake.

Cassie listened carefully. She tried to hear the yellow thrush that Uncle Fred had taught her to recognize last Thursday. Uncle Fred said that birds sang to arrange a gathering, that they sang for the joy of it, that they sang to tell each other where good berries were to be found. Cassie didn't believe him. Cassie thought the birds sang because they were lonely and calling to each other.

It was a nice day. She had to admit that, with the sun coming through her window touching her face. Cassie lay there, wondering how she was going to get through the weekend. Aunt Emily and Uncle Fred did have a TV, but it only got a couple of channels because they were so far out in the hills. And cable didn't even run out there, if you could believe it. And they didn't (of course!) have a VCR.

One of the channels they did get was public television, which Aunt Emily loved.

Great, Cassie thought. Now I can watch a solid morning of news programs or nature shows. Something educational, just what I want.

"Hey, lazy bones," Uncle Fred called. "When are you going to get up?"

Cassie groaned and pulled her body out of bed.

There were pleasant smells coming from the kitchen. I guess I have to get dressed, she thought. She put on her jeans and her *Save the Whales* T-shirt.

"So, want to help us in the garden?" Uncle Fred asked at breakfast. He had already made a huge pile of blueberry pancakes, which were sitting on the counter. He looked completely awake, while Aunt Emily sat there, staring out the window at nothing. Cassie wondered if Aunt Emily was mad at her. Cassie wondered what time she'd gotten to bed the night before. Maybe she'd never gotten to bed? Maybe she'd danced the whole night and was tired and that's why she wasn't talking?

"So, how many pancakes do you want?" Uncle Fred was asking.

Even Cassie had to admit that they looked good. "A couple, thanks."

"So, how about the garden? I'm harvesting the last of the tomatoes, and I'm going down to Landerson's to get some horse manure. Gil promised me a load yesterday." Uncle Fred took a deep breath and kept talking. "Boy, after that load I put in last year, our worms did *great*! I found some that were a foot, I'm telling you, Emily, a foot long. Do you know how good that is for the garden?"

"Ummm, yes dear. You've told me many times before."

"So, how about it, Cassie?" Uncle Fred said. "Want to come with me to get the manure?"

Cassie never expected that! The sickness that had

been lurking in her earlier that morning came back. "No, I . . . no, I don't feel that good."

"Are you sick?" Uncle Fred started coming toward her.

"No, I'm okay, it's just that I . . . I don't like to do a lot in the morning. I'm kind of tired."

"Ah, you're just like your aunt. Looks like I'm still the only morning person in the family." He returned to making more pancakes.

Cassie didn't tell him that, at home, she got up with lots of energy. She watched him at the stove, hoping he'd forget about the manure trip.

"So, I can't convince you to come with me?" Uncle Fred asked.

"Maybe Cassie doesn't like manure," Aunt Emily said, suddenly sitting up in her chair, as though she'd been poked.

Uncle Fred looked a little hurt. "Well, maybe she'd like to come for the ride."

"Ummm."

"What *would* you like to do, Cassie?"

"Well, uh . . . is there a mall around here?"

"A mall? No, there's one in Holyoke, but that's over an hour away."

"Hey, I got a great idea," Uncle Fred said. "You can go wading up at Puffet's."

Aunt Emily seemed to actually wake up. She appeared almost enthusiastic about the idea. "That's right, it's a warm day. You'll love it. You walk up the road to Brennar's Dairy Farm and then take a right on the dirt road past the farmhouse, and then it's a quarter mile down on the left."

The idea of walking up a dirty road and wading in a dirty pond seemed truly horrible to Cassie. But then, she thought about the foot-long worms in the garden and, even worse, the manure trip. She tried to look enthusiastic.

"Well, uh . . . ," Cassie said. "I like water."

"Then that will be fun for you," Uncle Fred said. He brought the pile of pancakes over and set them down in the center of the table.

They were delicious. Thank goodness Cassie liked something here!

After breakfast, she went and got her suit on and came back to the kitchen to say good-bye. Aunt Emily was still sitting quietly, staring at nothing.

" 'Bye, Aunt Emily," Cassie said. "I hope you . . . I . . ."

Aunt Emily turned toward her quickly, and Cassie forgot what she was trying to say.

"Better put on long pants over your suit," Uncle Fred said. "Or the bugs will eat you alive up there."

"Good-bye," said Cassie, quickly leaving before Uncle Fred could change his mind and make her go on the manure trip.

Another example of the wonderful, wholesome country, Cassie thought, remembering Uncle Fred's bug comment, as she trudged up the road. There was nothing around, only pastures and cows and hills of trees beyond the pastures. She could stand it if only there was at least a little store around. She figured that she could cash in her bank account and eat Snickers Bars for a year.

Cassie remembered one of her last weekends at home. She'd woken up early and watched cartoons playing softly so they wouldn't wake her mom.

Around ten, her mom had gotten up and they'd sat in the kitchen together, Cassie's mom having her Saturday mug of coffee and Cassie drinking an extra large glass of orange juice. When they were fully awake, after an hour or so, the cleaning had begun. They'd turned the stereo on — loud — and spent their weekly hour cleaning the apartment.

Cassie had cleaned the bathroom and had done the dusting, and her mom had done the vacuuming. Then they'd gone for lunch down at Amberdian's, where Cassie always got a cheeseburger — rare — with fries. Cassie used to like Saturday mornings.

That morning on the mountain, it was easy for Cassie to find the farmhouse because she and Mom had walked up there that last day when Mom had left her. Cassie turned onto the dirt road toward the pond.

Suddenly, she felt empty. She felt terrified. She wanted her mother. For an instant, she thought that a bear might come out of the woods or, worse still, a snake. But then she reminded herself that Uncle

Fred had told her there weren't any poisonous snakes around there. The winters were too cold for them.

A hundred miles south or so, there were copperheads and rattlesnakes. What if one of them traveled north by mistake? What if some were being taken up here to a zoo and they escaped? What if . . . ?

Cassie's fingers felt numb, and then something deep in her chest froze. She held her breath a long time and looked around for a place to run. But there was no refuge, no safety, no familiar sight; only the road going up and the road going down and woods on either side.

Trying to relax her hands, Cassie forced herself to keep walking up the road. Her mom always told her that when she got scared, really scared, she should concentrate on how her feet felt beneath her. If she were sitting, she should put her feet flat on the floor and wiggle her toes and look around and notice things. If she were walking, she should think about how it felt to put her weight on each foot, and then she should hold herself up straight and look around.

Okay. Clunk. Clunk. Pat. Pat. There's a tree and another and over there's a little flower . . . it's pretty . . . and that's a birch tree. It's shining in the sun, and there's one of those little stone walls set back from the road. Uncle Fred said this land used to be cleared. There were farms up here when the settlers came up to the hills to get away from the Indians in the valley. Oh, and here's a little stone. It's so round, and smooth. How come? It's like a stone by the ocean. How could a little stone get so round and smooth up here? On a mountain.

Cassie picked up the stone and looked at it carefully. It was white with tiny flecks of a mustard color. It was pretty, and Cassie almost put it in her pocket to take home. But then she remembered that it was her mom who had taught her to do this, her mom who had taught her to look around and notice things when she was scared. Cassie closed her fingers tightly against the stone and threw it into the woods. She threw it hard.

She found the pond. It was right near the road. She couldn't miss it.

It was small, tiny, Cassie thought. It was a no-big-deal pond. The pond in the park back home was bigger, and it had ducks in it you could feed. And it had a mowed grassy area you could have a picnic on.

This pond didn't have any nice grass. It did have one flat area leading up to it, with dirt and gravel and stones and nothing growing on it. That seemed strange in the woods: to have a place with nothing growing on it.

On the opposite side to where Cassie stood were big trees and, close to the pond, an area of cattails. Some tall, wild grasses were turning yellow at the edge of the pond, and some little flowers that Cassie had never seen before grew to the right of the gravel area. The wind blew and brought the smell of a pine forest to Cassie. She shivered — it was a smell she somehow remembered from an unknown past. She shivered again and clenched her hands together.

This is what's supposed to be so great, Cassie thought. This is what's supposed to be much more interesting than a mall. I mean, it's kind of pretty, but . . .

"And I'm not going wading in a snake infested pit," she said out loud. "Besides, wading is for babies."

"There's no snakes in that pond," someone said behind her.

Cassie jumped. "Oh!"

"Mr. Brennar dozes it out ever year so it's clean for everybody."

Cassie turned. A boy was standing behind her, a boy smaller than her, with deep brown hair blown around on his head. He had the greenest eyes Cassie had ever seen.

"I didn't mean to scare you, or nothing."

"No, I . . ."

"Hi, I'm Ernie, Ernie Bartos. I live up over the top of the hill." He stuck out his hand in a friendly and very adult way, and Cassie shook it.

"I'm Cassie Hannely. It's Cassandra really, but everybody calls me Cassie. I'm living with my Aunt Emily and Uncle Fred."

"I figured it was you, you being a stranger around here. Nice to meet you."

"Nice to meet you, too." Cassie meant it. Ernie, at least, was talking to her, even if he was only a little kid.

"Want to skip some stones?"

"Okay." Cassie wasn't really sure what that meant, but Ernie was already bending down and getting a round, flat stone from the ground. He threw it onto the pond with a wide, side swing of his arm. The stone touched on the water and then seemed to jump and land again, only to jump for a second and third and a fourth time. The circles in the water reached into each other. "Hey, that's pretty good!"

"Want to try one?" Ernie handed her a stone.

"How do I do it?"

"You stand like this and swing wide. You just try to hit the top of the water."

Cassie's first stone kerplunked with a splash, and they both laughed. But by her fifth try, she was pretty good, and she and Ernie stayed at the pond a long time, skipping stones.

"This is a pretty one," Cassie said, handing a rather large stone to Ernie. It had flecks of shininess in it, and she could peel off some of it with her fingernail.

"That's mica. I have lots of it in my collection."

"You have a rock collection?"

"Yeah, I have granite and garnet and marble and even some pyrite I bought. You can come up and see 'em at my house if you want."

"Oh, I don't know."

"Only if you want to, I mean."

"Yeah, sure, I'd like to, but I'm supposed to be back for lunch pretty soon."

"I didn't mean today, I meant sometime."

"Oh. Thanks. Yeah, I'd like that."

"I gotta go. I gotta help my father chop wood this afternoon."

"Hey, Ernie. How do you like living in the country?"

"I don't know. I like it. We moved here two years ago from Putney, but that was country, too, so there's no difference." He started to walk up the path to the road.

"I guess I'll see you at school."

"Yeah."

"You take the school bus?"

"Yeah, they pick me up before they get you. I've seen you get on."

It felt funny to Cassie to now actually know one of the faces that had been staring at her. "What grade you in?" she asked.

"Nice meeting you," Ernie said, as he quickly walked away.

"Well, see ya. Thanks for teaching me how to skip stones," she yelled after him. She meant it. She'd had a good time. For about an hour, she'd forgotten all about her mother deciding to go full time to college.

She stayed around the pond for a while, and then

walked back to the house. Loretta, Aunt Emily's friend, was over visiting, having tea in the kitchen. They both got quiet when Cassie walked in. Her mom's second letter was waiting for her on the counter, and Cassie took it to her bedroom to read.

My darling Cassie,

How are you? I haven't gotten your first letter yet. I wish I could call, but I've got to save those pennies. Maybe I can call on my birthday.

I love school. It's so much easier, you can't believe it. Remember how I used to have to stay up so late? Now, I go to class and work in the library all day, and then get home by 4:30 and make Mrs. Schneider her supper. It's really easy, all she'll eat is hamburgers and pork chops and simple things like that.

And, would you believe it, the only vegetable she'll eat is canned string beans, boiled for at least twenty minutes — YUCK! And she has Pop Tarts for breakfast and a peanut butter and jelly sandwich for lunch. I don't know how she's gotten to be this old, unless she's really forty and pretending to be eighty-seven (ha, ha!).

So, I was telling you about my day. So, I have supper with Mrs. Schneider at ex-

actly five-thirty (she's a stickler for timing) and then we watch the six o'clock news, and then I hit the books again for a couple more hours. But it's so easy! Last night, I got to bed by nine! I feel like I'm in heaven.

How are you eating? I sent Aunt Emily and Uncle Fred your favorite lasagna recipe. Do you have enough clothes? Did you remember to tell Aunt Emily that you need to get your teeth cleaned next month? How's school?

Love and kisses and hundreds of hugs,
Your mother who misses you like crazy

The part about the lasagna recipe made Cassie feel really bad. She knew that they'd *never* put the sausage in the recipe, never in a million years. Didn't Mom *know* they were vegetarians? Didn't she check them out before she made her live with them? And the sausage was the *best part*, the part that made it special.

Mom never wanted to see them before. She always said it was too far to visit. How come she thought they were so great now? How come she thought it was such a great place for Cassie to live, now, just when she wanted to get rid of Cassie for a year?

Maybe it was for more than a year. Maybe she wasn't ever coming back.

Dear Mom,
Mrs. Schneider sounds nice. I'm glad you like school. I . . .

Cassie scrunched it up and got it in the trash with one toss.

Dear Mom,
How come you hate me? How come you don't want me anymore? Did I do something wrong? I know it's my fault that you left. Did I make you mad?
Maybe if I'd worked harder in school and like done the dishes more, without complaining I mean, then maybe you wouldn't have been so tired and then you could have worked and finished up school in Boston. I'm sorry I didn't work harder, Mom.
I shouldn't have asked for that painting set for Christmas last year because it was so expensive and you bought it anyway and that's why you thought we needed more money so you had to go back to school, full time. Please come home, Mom. Please . . . I'll get a job baby-sitting or something. I'm old enough now, and I'll make lots of money for us and I'll . . .

It had made sense while she was writing it, but it sounded funny when she read it back. She picked up the teddy bear, the one that had been left in her room when she'd come that first day, and held him close.

This time, Cassie did cry after she threw the letter away.

Chapter Four

Cassie was almost glad to be back at school.

On Sunday, Aunt Emily and Uncle Fred had taken her to a Baroque concert in Vermont. To get there, they'd driven through hundreds of hills with thousands of trees, and Aunt Emily kept raving about the beautiful scenery. Cassie didn't have anything against trees, but she thought that they all looked the same: leafy and green, green and leafy, what was the big deal?

Uncle Fred had kept talking about getting more manure for the garden, and every time they passed a new house that was facing the road instead of facing the southern sun, he had a fit. "That's absolutely disgusting," he would say. "A new house, and all that new technology, and they don't even face it to the sun. Well, if they want to live in a dark, cold house, it's up to them. Wasteful!"

"Yes, dear," Aunt Emily would say.

On that Monday morning, the rows of math problems facing Cassie on her desk were at least something to do, and she actually did like the feel of the classroom, a large, open room with windows reaching, it seemed, from the floor to the high ceiling. She could look right out and see the sloping lawn and the woods, beginning just beyond the soccer field.

In South Braintree, she'd gone to a modern school with the regulation ceilings and smaller windows. The bigger scale of Northwood made her think of mystery, that there was mystery in the world, even somewhere in Northwood Elementary School.

Structure and houses and rooms and space interested Cassie. Her mom had once wanted to be an architect, and she'd taught Cassie about salt boxes and colonials and gable roofs and turrets. In South Braintree, on cloudy Sunday afternoons, they'd walk past the rows of tenements and the neighborhoods of white clapboard two- and three-story homes. They'd walk to a good part of town, like Washington Street, and look at houses.

Cassie's favorite was a huge old place overlooking a pond. Its five pillars and porch across the front made her think of a southern mansion. Imagine that! A southern mansion in South Braintree, Massachusetts.

Cassie shook her head, suddenly seeing the math problems on her desk and Mrs. Kalish at the chalkboard. She wasn't in South Braintree. She was in Northwood Elementary and, on that Monday morning, Mrs. Kalish was teaching them about multiplying fractions.

The girl with the ponytail sitting next to Cassie turned and whispered to her, "This is so boring."

Cassie shrugged. She was trying to hear what Mrs. Kalish was saying.

The girl went on. "So how come you sit in the front of the bus with the little kids?"

"I don't know. I don't *know* anybody."

"Yeah, but the rule is, if you're a sixth-grader, you sit in the back. It is absolutely not cool to sit in the front."

"Why?"

"It's just not cool. Don't you know anything?"

"I've never taken a school bus before."

"Never?"

"No, we lived in the city."

"Well, I don't mean to be mean or anything, but the kids are starting to make fun of you 'cause you're sitting up front."

Cassie felt her forehead getting hot. She'd never been popular at school before, but she'd never been laughed at, either. And she and Lauren and Tara had always walked back and forth to school together, ever since they'd been in first grade.

"Don't worry," the girl was saying. "I'll save you a seat this afternoon, and that'll stop that."

"Wow, thanks."

"No problem. . . . I'm Cora."

"I'm Cassie."

"I know."

"How?"

"You're new. Everybody around here knows your name. You're living with your Aunt Emily and Uncle Fred for the year."

Cassie was amazed. "How'd you know *that*?"

"My mom takes aerobics with Sally Matten, and she works at the clinic with your aunt. Besides," Cora laughed, "when I grow up, I'm going to be a Doctor of Gossip."

Cassie laughed, too. Maybe Cora wasn't so bad, after all. She looked up, directly into Cora's face this time, and noticed her pretty blue eyes and slightly large nose. She wondered if the kids had ever made fun of Cora because of it. In her old school, some of the kids used to call one girl "beakface." Cassie hated it when they did.

Mrs. Kalish interrupted their conversation. "Please pass your math papers in, and we're going to do some creative writing."

The same thing happened this time. Nobody groaned. Not one person put his finger in his mouth, pretending like he was going to throw up. What was with these kids? Cassie couldn't figure it out.

"This will be another small assignment," Mrs. Kalish said. "We'll start on fables and folk tales at some point, but for now, you can write on anything you want."

Cassie was glad that, now, she had somebody to ask. And having the desks that close did make it easier. "How come?" she whispered to Cora.

"How come what?"

"How come nobody hates writing in this school?"

Cora leaned back in her chair. "I don't know. I guess we're used to it. We've always just done it, ever since kindergarten."

"Really?"

"Yeah, I mean, I have this stupid little book from kindergarten where I drew pictures of our cows and Mr. Dicenso, he was our teacher then, he typed each cow's name on the bottom."

"You have cows?"

But Cora didn't answer because Mrs. Kalish was looking at them. She paused, then took a deep breath and said, "Any questions before you get started?"

"Can you give us an idea?" Anthony asked.

"Do you need one?"

Several kids said yes. But still, they weren't complaining. They were just sitting, watching Mrs. Kalish.

"Okay, if you want, you could start by saying, 'I woke up on Saturday to find the rhino in my bathtub.' "

A few kids laughed, and Cassie sat numbly, watching a whole room of kids settling down to write. Some of them looked like they even had special notebooks they were taking out of their desks.

Mrs. Kalish paused for a minute as she handed Cassie a piece of paper. "All set?" she asked.

Cassie shrugged. "What if I can't spell some-thing?"

"Don't worry about it. Do the best you can. I don't burn people at the stake for spelling a word wrong." She smiled.

Cassie didn't know what else to do, so she started writing. After twenty minutes or so, she'd written:

> *When I woke up that Saturday, the rhino was in my bathtub. Again. The last time, he'd gotten in by smashing through the living room wall, but this time, there was no sign of how he got there.*
>
> *He sat there, staring at me. He lifted up his head and blew soap bubbles at me. That was too much. I grabbed my shampoo and squirted some at him. "Thanks," he said, "put some on my back, will you? I'm having a dandruff problem."*

Cassie was interrupted by Mrs. Kalish. "If you want, you can do peer conferences now."

"What's that mean?" she asked Cora.

"We can work together. You want to?" Rather than waiting for Cassie's answer, Cora reached over and took Cassie's paper off her desk. Cassie sat, stunned. All of a sudden, Cora was laughing. "Hey, this is pretty good. Listen to this." She'd turned and was reading Cassie's story to Sarah and Margy.

Cassie couldn't breathe. She clenched her hands together.

But then, Sarah and Margy were laughing. "I like how you said the rhino was having a dandruff problem."

"You do?"

"You're pretty good," Sarah said.

"You're funny," Margy said.

"I am?" Cassie couldn't believe it. No one in the whole world had ever called her funny before.

After school, Cora did save her a seat in the back of the bus. It felt different to walk straight past the rows of kids, all talking and laughing. On that Monday afternoon, it suddenly seemed that nobody was staring at her anymore. They didn't seem to even notice her.

As she walked by, Cassie saw Ernie sitting in the midsection of the bus, where the medium-sized kids sat. Cassie said hi to him, and he said hi back, but it seemed like he didn't really want to talk to her. That's probably because she was a sixth-grader, and he was one of the littler kids.

Cassie kept walking to the back, trying to pretend that she'd done it many times before. But she was glad when she finally reached Cora and slid in next to her. "Thanks," she said.

Cora didn't say anything. She just handed her a piece of gum.

Dear Mom,
    I wrote a story in school today. I . . .

Dear Mom,
    I . . .

Cassie got up from her bed and walked around the room. She picked up the teddy bear and stuffed him face down on the bed. Then she felt bad and picked him up and placed him nicely on her pillow.

Mom wanted a letter? She wanted a stupid old letter? Fine, she'd give her a letter.

Dear Mom,
    There are rats in my room and cock-roaches and . . .

Mom would never believe it. She'd seen the house that horrible Sunday when she'd dropped her off.

    . . . Uncle Fred smokes and Aunt Emily makes me work all the time and they lock me in my room and . . . they lock me in my room and . . . they don't give me any-thing I like to eat (there was some truth to that one — thank goodness for school lunches) . . . and they never let me watch TV and . . .

Dear Mom,

I found a rat in my room yesterday. It was eighteen inches long and it had bad breath. I know because it jumped on my bed while I was waking up and breathed on me. The rats around here have halitosis really bad. It must be something about this great country air.

Cassie almost laughed. She picked up the teddy bear and held him close. Then she crumpled up the letters.

She didn't make the basket with the last one. It lay there, unfolding and alone in the corner.

"The famous Larry Bird misses a shot at the buzzer," Cassie said out loud to no one.

Chapter Five

Dear Cassie,

What's wrong? I haven't heard from you. Aunt Emily says you're doing fine. She's written twice.

Mrs. Schneider is turning out to be a real pain. Now she's decided that she'll only eat fried chicken for supper, with french fries and her horrible canned string beans. And she's demanding that I make her brownies every day, a whole pan. She needs them for snacks, she says, during the day when I'm gone. I don't mind making them, it's not that, but her diet is so awful, I hate being a part of it. She says that it's none of my business. Maybe she's right.

I still like school. I'm taking Sociology of Aging (cute professor, easy course), The Modern Novel (tons of books to read and even more papers — HELP, I'm being smothered by an avalanche of papers!), Psychology of Learning, Advanced Psy-

chology of Aging, and Chemistry (Yuck —
I hate it.) I wish it wasn't a requirement.
Yesterday, I was boiling a beaker of chemicals, and it got boiling so hard, the beaker
started shaking. It shook so much, it fell
and smashed on the table, all over the lab.
Every time I come in the lab now, the assistant (this child — a giant child of 6'4" and
probably all of twenty-two years old) tells
me to be careful. I mean, it was an accident!
It could have happened to anybody. Am I
going to be labeled a "Laboratory Destruc-
tor" for the rest of my life?

Well, I've got to go. This has turned out
to be a long letter. Speaking of letters, you
don't have to write me a long one. It can
be short, and don't worry about spelling or
anything like that. I know this man who
went away to prep school for junior high.
Whenever he wrote his father a letter, his
father would correct all his errors and send
it back to him. I'd never do that to you. I
just want to hear from you, even a postcard
would be okay.

I love you tons and tons.

Your loving,
Mom

"Cassie, I got a great letter from your Mom," Aunt
Emily said, "I see you got one, too."

Cassie shrugged, not looking up from the TV. She was watching a M*A*S*H rerun.

"She says you haven't written."

Cassie shrugged again, leaning over this time and grabbing Newsweek from the coffee table. That was a mistake. Aunt Emily knew she wasn't interested in that magazine.

Aunt Emily came and sat next to her on the couch, and Cassie moved away from her.

"Do you need help getting started? Here, I saw this great stationery at Kartlet's and I thought you might like it." She showed Cassie the box of stationery she'd bought that afternoon. Every notecard had a brightly colored cat sitting in front of a bouquet of flowers and fruit.

"I have paper," Cassie said.

"Don't you like it? I bought it for you." She tried to hand it to Cassie, but Cassie moved away ever so slightly and turned another page of Newsweek.

"Cassie, what's the problem? It's been two weeks and you haven't written her once."

"I don't know."

"Here, why don't you get your pen and paper and start a letter now. You can work on the kitchen table while I start supper."

"I'm tired."

"I want you to start one now, just start one." Aunt Emily's voice had a new tone, a tone that made Cassie mad.

She put *Newsweek* back on the coffee table and stood up. She started to leave.

"Shut that TV off, please. Where are you going?"

Cassie didn't answer. She just kept walking.

"Come back here, young lady." Aunt Emily's voice was sharp. Mom never talked to her like that. "Come back here! You can't run away from your problems."

"Watch me." Cassie said under her breath, but she stopped and turned. Aunt Emily looked mean, mean and ugly at that moment. Cassie hated her.

"Cassie, I . . . Cassie, I'm sorry I yelled. I . . . look, come and sit down here on the couch. Look, I'll sit over here." Aunt Emily sat in the big rocker next to the fireplace.

"I don't want to."

Aunt Emily sighed. It looked like she held her breath for a moment and then slowly let it out. Somehow, Cassie noticed that she was even wiggling her toes. "All right," she finally said. "We'll talk here. Look, your mother's worried about you. She just wants to know you're all right. Why don't you go get your notepaper and I'll help you."

"No."

"I'll help you get started. I know it's hard to get started."

"No."

"Cassie — "

"No, I don't want to. I don't want to." She felt like she might cry.

It was really lucky that the phone rang just then. Aunt Emily didn't say anything more, just sat there, listening to the phone ring. It rang five times, and then she got up to answer it. It was Loretta.

It was a warm September afternoon, so Cassie went out the sliding door to the porch and then out to the driveway. She walked to the pond. Ernie was there already.

"I'll beat ya," he said. "No more Mr. Nice Guy, you know how to do it now." He picked up a flat stone and skipped it over the water. "First one to reach twenty-one wins."

"Twenty-one skips?"

"Yeah. Whaddaya think?"

Cassie laughed. "You don't have a chance. They call me Killer Skipper."

"Put your rock where your mouth is." He picked up another stone. "Okay, I'm first."

"Who says?"

"We got a legal eagle in the group, folks. Okay, I'll throw and then you, and then the one who gets most skips goes first."

"Okay, that's fair."

"Go for it."

Ernie beat her on the first set, but she won the second and the third. He clobbered her on the fourth, and then she had a comeback on the fifth. It was so much fun not to think about school or her mother or Aunt Emily for that little bit of time.

Dear Mom,

I had fun at the pond. I've got a friend up there. He's only in fourth grade, but he's nice. Is it okay to have a friend who's younger than you? And a boy?"

For a moment, it seemed like she was really talking to her mother, like her mother was really there. That made Cassie mad.

The scrunched up letter had found its home in the wastebasket, along with the others, when Aunt Emily knocked on the door.

Cassie stuffed her notepad and pen under her blanket and stood up. "Come in."

Aunt Emily didn't come in slowly this time. She came in quickly, like she had a reason to be there. All of a sudden, she was next to the wastebasket and picking it up. Then she was reaching for the crumpled-up letter in the corner.

"Trash day," she said. "From now on, why don't you bring this out every — "

"Don't touch that!" It was her loud voice, her real voice, her real voice when she was yelling. She reached for the basket, almost grabbing it out of Aunt Emily's hands. She missed by a couple of inches because Aunt Emily pulled it away.

Aunt Emily stared at her.

Cassie felt suddenly terrified.

Aunt Emily gasped and put the basket down. "What's the matter, honey?" She looked down into the basket. Maybe she saw the letters. Maybe she even saw what one of them said. "Oh." She bent down and touched the side of the basket and then moved it quickly toward Cassie. "Well," she said, "it's not really full, no sense taking this out yet. When it's full, really full, why don't you bring it out into the kitchen and empty it into the trash barrel out there."

She turned quickly and walked out. Cassie was left, staring at nothing, a tear waiting on her cheek.

Chapter Six

The following Thursday in the late afternoon, Cassie was standing in the kitchen. One of them, probably Aunt Emily, had brought Cassie's notepad into the kitchen and put it on the table. It was her special notepad, the Far Side one that Mom had bought her, the one that had the dinosaurs on the bottom smoking cigarettes.

It was her special notepad, and they had no business touching it. And they especially had no business going into her room and bringing it into the kitchen.

Uncle Fred was sitting at the table, writing. Motioning for Cassie to sit down in the chair next to him, he showed her what he was working on.

It was a fill-in-the-blanks letter.

> Dear _____,
>   I am _____. The weather is _____.
> Uncle Fred is _____. Aunt Emily is
> nicer, of course.
>   I _____ school. I'm learning about
> _____ and _____. My teach-
> er's name is _____. Would you be-

*lieve me if I told you that, at this school, I
need lots of money for field trips? Next
week, we're going to the* _____ *and*
_____ . *Please send money, lots of
money.*

Your loving _____ ,

_____

He handed it to Cassie with a smile, and she
laughed, in spite of herself. Aunt Emily laughed, too,
standing at the sink washing vegetables.

"Don't, please don't tell her about us making you
eat brussel sprouts for breakfast! And don't, whatever you do, for heaven's sake, don't tell her about
the Television Torture."

Cassie looked up. Uncle Fred had a grimace on
his face.

"The Television Torture," he was saying. "Think
of it! A contemporary child, an eleven-year-old,
being forced to live in a home where the TV only
gets two channels. And one . . . one of them . . .
this is the awful part, folks, . . . one of them is . . .
PUBLIC TV!" He slid off his chair and to the floor,
holding his stomach.

Cassie knew he was trying to be funny. She knew
he was trying to make her laugh. But, suddenly all
she wanted was to get out of the kitchen. She looked
toward the door. But they were watching her.

"Do you think you'll be okay getting started?"
Uncle Fred asked. He motioned toward the notepad.

Cassie didn't answer.

"You want some help?"

"No."

"Why don't you just try," Aunt Emily said.

Cassie felt almost sick, sitting at the kitchen table with the empty dinosaur notepad in front of her. She drew hats on the dinosaurs and filled in their cigarettes. Suddenly, it seemed that the dinosaurs were laughing at her.

Maybe if Aunt Emily was making something nice, maybe if she was making meat loaf and mashed potatoes and corn, frozen corn, the kind Cassie liked, maybe then she could have started. But sitting there, watching Aunt Emily buttering the soufflé pan and getting the broccoli out of the refrigerator, Cassie felt her stomach growing tight.

"Oh, my goodness," Aunt Emily was saying, as she was examining the broccoli stalks that Uncle Fred had harvested from the garden, "I'd better soak these good. Here are three cabbage worms!" She held up a little green worm for Cassie to see.

"You mean," Cassie heard her voice asking, "there're worms in there?"

"Don't worry, the salt kills them. Besides," she laughed, "if we eat one or two, it's added protein."

Cassie's heart felt low in her body. She looked down at the paper and had a sudden urge to crumple it up, but then she looked up to see Aunt Emily watching her again. She picked up her pen.

"You could tell her about our trip to Vermont."

Right, Cassie thought. Aunt Emily and Uncle Fred had thought it was a big deal to go to this granite quarry on Sunday. It had been some fun to go on the little train into the quarry, but the ride only lasted ten minutes and it wasn't even scary. Cassie looked down again. Somehow, she couldn't make herself start writing. The pen felt heavy, and her fingers were tired.

"I have to go to the bathroom," she said, as though she needed permission to get up from the table.

"Well go ahead, but come right back, please," Aunt Emily said.

She was right. She did need permission.

Cassie came back after a few minutes and sat back down at the table. Aunt Emily wasn't even in the kitchen anymore, but Uncle Fred was at the counter making blueberry muffins. What were they doing? Taking shifts as guards?

"Hey, sweetie," he said. "If you need any help at all, just ask."

No answer.

"How about you tell her about your room, or school or something?"

No answer.

Uncle Fred sighed.

They can make me sit here, Cassie thought. But they can't make me write. She tightened her lips and rested her chin on her closed fist.

She sat, for an hour it seemed, smelling the soufflé

cooking, smelling the blueberry muffins baking, listening to Aunt Emily and Uncle Fred sitting out in the living room now, and talking. She hated them.

She hated her mother.

She suddenly remembered that there'd been broccoli in the quiche Aunt Emily had made last night. She'd eaten some, she'd had to, they'd been watching her. But she'd turned her head and hadn't chewed.

What if there'd been cabbage worms in that quiche? What if they'd survived Aunt Emily's salt bath? And she hadn't chewed very well.

Cassie closed her eyes and saw hundreds, maybe thousands of the cabbage worms. Great, she thought. By now they are probably setting up homes in my stomach. They're building cabbage worm colonials and condominiums and little shops, even, where they buy what they can't produce in my stomach. They're building malls with movie houses and roller skating rinks, and roadways from one part of my body to another.

All of a sudden, she felt really sick. But she did make it to the bathroom before she threw up.

They didn't make her eat supper. Around seven, Aunt Emily brought her some toast and a light soup, but Cassie couldn't eat. Her stomach felt green, cabbage worm green.

She dreamt many dreams that night, but lots of them starred little green creatures, little green creatures who looked like cabbage worms.

They were in her desk at school, and some of them were in her sandwich, but they talked to her so she knew they were there before she ate them. They grew in size. One of them asked if she wanted to be friends and she said yes. Then all of a sudden, she was crying.

Cassie woke up in the morning, tired. She was surprised to discover, though, that someone had come in during the night and put the large quilt from the living room over her. It was the good quilt, the log cabin quilt, the one that Aunt Emily had made that she was so proud of. Cassie didn't think anybody ever used it. She thought it was supposed to stay draped over the couch, just for show. Cassie didn't know if she was embarrassed or grateful, but, somehow, it made it easier to face them that next morning.

Chapter Seven

Cassie waited numbly for the school bus. She climbed the stairs without thinking when it groaned to a stop, and nodded to Mr. G when he saluted her broadly, touching the rim of his red plaid hat. He smiled at her, like he always did.

"Entrée, my dear Cassandra," he said. "It's a pleasure to have you aboard. I hope your stay with us will be pleasant and rewarding."

Usually, Cassie laughed at his jokes. But not this morning.

She was looking toward the back, hoping to see Cora in their spot. At first, she didn't see her. Maybe she wasn't there. Maybe she was sick or something. Maybe there wouldn't be a seat saved for her this morning.

Aha, but no, there Cora was. She'd just turned her head for a moment.

But then Cassie's foot slipped. She almost fell, when Ernie was suddenly there, grabbing her elbow, holding her up. He smiled.

Cassie stood on her own feet again. She looked around. She didn't think that anyone else saw it happen. The kids were talking and looking out the windows. Cassie smiled back at Ernie and thanked him with her eyes. Then she kept on walking back to Cora.

"You look awful," Cora said, as Cassie slumped into her seat.

"Thanks."

"No, I mean it. What's wrong?"

Cassie shrugged. She certainly didn't want to tell Cora about last night. She wanted to forget it.

"Is it *them*?" Cora was asking. "Are they making you eat weird food and sleep with tapes on in your room so that you get brainwashed?"

"Huh?"

"You know, so that you start believing something weird, like *them*."

"No, it's nothing like that."

"My mother said that she saw your aunt in the IGA yesterday, and your aunt was asking if there were pesticides in the *milk*."

Cassie's heart sank. Until now, she was hoping that only she knew how weird Aunt Emily was.

Cora was continuing, as she always did. "And Mr. Blackstone was telling her that their milk comes from Landerson's, and that farm has been here for generations, and he'd grown up on that milk and his children have grown up on that milk, and it was fine, thank you very much, just fine, and why was she always asking so many questions?"

Cassie groaned.

"And then your aunt said that she'd read this article that if cows eat sprayed fields, the pesticides get in the milk. Mr. Blackstone told her that those fields have never been sprayed and never will be, because in the first place, it's too expensive and in the second place there's no need. Then your Aunt Emily said that she was relieved. She said that now, of course, she had to be extra careful because she had a new young person to feed."

"She said *that!*"

"Verbatim. My mother told me she said, 'a new young person to feed.' "

"Oh, gross!" Cassie groaned a second time that morning.

"And your aunt was wearing that long purple cape that she has, with the flower fabric for a lining, and she had on jeans and a silk shirt."

Cassie didn't groan this time. It was too awful. She had seen the cape for the first time last Wednesday and, already, after only being here for a few weeks, she knew that it wasn't something you were supposed to wear to get milk at the IGA. You were supposed to wear T-shirts and jeans, or corduroy pants and flannel shirts, or if a grown-up was getting home from work she could have on a simple dress. Sensible clothes, she thought, you were supposed to wear sensible clothes to the IGA.

"They made me eat tofu this weekend," Cassie heard herself telling Cora. "Tofu and string beans with a ginger sauce."

"Isn't there a law against that? I mean, you're going to starve to death."

"And last week, we had . . . " Cassie leaned closer to Cora so no one would hear. "Last week, we had lentil loaf."

"Ugh, barf city," Cora said. "Maybe I can bring you some of the leftover meat loaf we had last night."

"Would you? I'd kill for meat loaf! I've been living on peanut butter, and I'm really sick of it."

"I'll try. I'm sure my mother'll let me."

Somehow, that made Cassie feel better, and she took a deep breath and looked out the window. All of a sudden, she was aware that instead of going straight down West Mountain like they usually did, Mr. G was taking a quick right turn onto Wolf's Den Road. He drove for half a mile down, and then stopped the bus in front of a graying farmhouse with a porch that wrapped itself around two sides. There were three huge pine trees growing in what Cassie thought used to be the yard. Now, it was all goldenrod and small bushes. There were still spots of color, here and there. Flowers, Cassie thought, flowers that stood for a time when the farm was cared for.

Mr. G honked the horn once and then twice. Cassie figured that they were picking up a new kid.

They waited for a few minutes, and then Mr. G honked the horn again. A tiny lady, all bent over and walking with a cane started out to the bus. She was all bundled up in a navy blue coat. She walked slowly.

"Hold your horses," she yelled, looking up at them. "You woke me out of a sound sleep."

"I can send out one of the kids to get it, Mrs. Parnelli," Mr. G said as she got near. "Now that the weather's getting cold."

"You're getting just like my children," she yelled, hitting the sides of the school bus stairs as she climbed up. It seemed to Cassie that she used her cane more to hit than to walk. "I'm not an invalid!"

She handed a piece of folded paper to Mr. G and then turned to look at them all. "Who's that?" she asked, and Cassie realized, with a shock, that she was pointing her cane at her.

"I said, who's that? Stand up, dearie, and tell me your name."

"Do it and get it over with," Cora whispered.

Cassie tried, but she felt glued to her seat. Mrs. Parnelli started down the aisle toward her. Cora poked her, and Cassie jumped up and said, "Cassie Hannely, ma'am. Nice to meet you."

Mrs. Parnelli stopped, and Cora grabbed Cassie's arm and pulled her down into her seat.

"New girl, huh?" Mrs. Parnelli said. "Looks okay. A little skinny, but looks okay. What are the rest of you gawking about?" She turned and marched down the aisle, hitting the side of each seat as she passed.

She thumped down the stairs and then went straight back to her house without looking back. Mr. G started the bus and drove off.

"Who *is* she?" Cassie asked.

"Oh, she's like that every year in the fall. She's grumpy because she just got back from her daughter's. She spends a month with her. She gets nice by October."

"But who *is* she?"

"We get groceries for her every Wednesday."

"*We* do?"

"No, not us, Mr. G. He gets 'em during the day. We'll stop by on the way home this afternoon."

"Won't he get in trouble?"

"What for?"

"Aren't there rules or something about Mr. G using the bus for personal errands?"

"It's not a personal errand. He's getting Mrs. Parnelli her groceries. Anyway, everybody helps her. The Saturday after Thanksgiving, my dad and a lot of other people go over and split and stack her wood for her for the winter. Your Aunt Emily and Uncle Fred were even there last year."

"They were?"

"Yeah, there must have been thirty people there. We had pizza afterward."

"But why can't she live with her daughter year round?"

"She could. She doesn't want to. And Mr. G says that, at her age, she should darn well be able to decide for herself where she's going to live."

Cassie was silent. She didn't understand a place where people helped an old lady who threatened people with her cane. It wasn't like she didn't have another place to live. It seemed to Cassie that Mrs. Parnelli was just being stubborn.

But Cora seemed to think it was normal. She wasn't saying anything sarcastic. She wasn't saying anything at all. She was sitting there, looking out the window. All the other kids were talking and laughing. Cassie could even see Ernie's head turned, talking to the kids in the seat behind him.

And then, from the front of the bus, came this truly weird sound. At first, Cassie didn't know what it was and none of the other kids seemed to notice. But there it was, even louder this time. It was Mr. G. He was singing, singing a song that Cassie had never heard. Somehow, she didn't want to ask Cora any more questions. But Cora just leaned over, all on her own, as if she knew that Cassie couldn't stand any more mysteries that morning.

"He's singing opera," she said, "the aria from *La Bohème*. He told us all about it last spring. He used to study opera in New York, when he was driving a cab for a living." Again, Cora made no sarcastic comment.

Cassie sighed and leaned back. She tried to close her eyes, but the ever-growing singing noises kept forcing them awake. She had heard opera before. Sometimes, on Saturday afternoons, Mom used to listen to it on the radio. But that hadn't sounded anything at all like Mr. G.

They did stop back at Mrs. Parnelli's that afternoon, laden with bags of groceries. All the kids had to step around the bags piled up near Mr. G, but no one complained.

Cassie almost talked to her mom in her mind as she walked past the bags and down the aisle, but then she stopped herself. If she *had* talked to her, she would have said, "Mom, how could you leave me trapped on this bus with a bus driver who sings opera and gets an old lady groceries on schooltime? And nobody cares? Everybody thinks he's normal?" If Cassie hadn't been so mad at her mom, that's what she certainly would have said.

> *Dear Mom,*
> *Thanks for leaving me in this wonderful place. It's so much fun meeting all these unusual people. I'm being culturally enriched. Just think, I'll turn into a . . .*

Cassie got out her scissors and cut the letter into tiny pieces, such tiny pieces that Aunt Emily'd never be able to read them.

Chapter Eight

"**C**assie, we're going to have to insist that you write your mother." Aunt Emily was sitting in the big rocker again that Saturday morning. Uncle Fred was standing by the fireplace. "We've talked it over, and we feel that you need us to insist."

"You can't make me."

"We don't want to have to make you."

"You can't make me. I won't. It's none of your business." Once she'd said it, her stomach tightened. She knew she wasn't supposed to talk to grown-ups like that.

But Aunt Emily wasn't yelling. "Sometimes in life we have to face things. It's time for you to do this. You're stuck . . . you're just stuck in your feelings." She was talking about her like she was some client.

"We agree on this, Cassie. We both feel this is right." Even Uncle Fred was against her.

They didn't care. They didn't care at all that she was miserable. They probably liked it. They probably talked about her all the time when they were in their room. They probably laughed at her.

"It only has to be a page, or even part of a page."

"No!" The word exploded. "No!" How would they like to leave their home and go to some strange place and have strangers boss them around, strangers who didn't care? "No!" The word was coming out of her easily now. She turned and left the living room, walking, purposely walking. She wouldn't let herself run.

Let them tell her to stop, Cassie thought. She wouldn't. They'd have to make her, they'd have to stop her physically. She wouldn't. She wouldn't do anything they wanted.

But silence stayed behind her and in front of her and filled her room, the silence of her pain. All morning, she lay on her bed staring at nothing.

She was amazed that they still let her go. Around one, Uncle Fred knocked on her door and told her he was ready to take her over to Cora's. They probably just wanted to get rid of her for the afternoon.

She and Uncle Fred rode in silence. Cassie was so glad that he didn't try to talk to her.

Cora lived on a farm, a working farm with cows and horses and sheep grazing in green, open pastures. Cora's family still had a milking herd. There were two long barns: modern ones, metal ones, not at all like the falling down gray barns Cassie had seen in pictures.

"Hey, Cora," her dad yelled from the doorway. "Give Cassie a tour."

Cassie didn't want a tour. She thought it would be smelly on a farm.

But the barn was okay, with cement floors that were clean, perfectly clean. None of the cows were in the barn that afternoon because it was a warm day and they were all out in the pasture.

Cora's dad was really proud of his milking machines. He showed Cassie a separate little room in the barn that housed a huge, gleaming machine. It was supposed to do something special with the milk, pasteurize it or something, Cassie thought. She didn't exactly understand what he said.

But she loved the kittens. There was a mother with three little babies near the barn door when she and Cora went back outside.

"They're five weeks old," Cora said.

"Can I pick them up?"

"Sure, if the mother doesn't scratch."

"You gonna keep 'em all?"

"You always do, on a farm. We need 'em to keep down the mice."

"Oh. But do they sleep with you and stuff?"

"Are you kidding? You really are a city kid. They live in the barn. They don't even go in the house." Cora laughed.

Suddenly, the kittens didn't seem as cute anymore. Cassie put down the black-and-white one she was holding, and the mother hissed at her.

"Hey, look, I'm giving it back." Cassie stood up quickly.

"But, if you ever wanted a kitten, you could have any one you want. You could even have that one." Cora sounded friendly again.

"Really?"

"Sure."

"I wonder if they'd let me have one?"

"You could ask."

"I don't know." Cassie didn't want to think about asking Aunt Emily and Uncle Fred for anything. In fact, on that sunny Indian summer Saturday with the wind blowing slightly, she didn't want to think about Aunt Emily and Uncle Fred at all.

They started walking along the west pasture toward the big white farmhouse that sat on a foundation of granite. Plants, rosebushes, and vines were growing over the porch.

"It's old," Cora told her. "My great-great grandfather built it, after the other place burned down."

"Wow."

"This farm has been in my family for hundreds of years, thousands even."

"Not thousands. Indians were here thousands of years ago."

"I know, but . . . we even got a burger named for us down at Addleson's. It's the quarter pounder with bacon and Swiss, but you can get American cheese if you want."

"C'mon."

"No really. They got sandwiches named after all

the farms around here. We can go sometime and have one."

"Really?" A burger sounded great.

"We even got a road named after us, Hodges Farm Road. It's because my ancestors were so smart to have moved to such a great place." Cora looked serious, but then she started laughing.

Cassie had never met anyone whose family had a road named after them. But still, she came from near Boston, and everybody knew that Boston was a pretty important place. "Well, you're not by the water, and you don't have great places like Faneuil Hall or really great places to shop like Filene's Basement."

"Well, we got Cartell's." They both laughed.

"And it's so much fun riding the T, you know, the train. We used to go into Boston practically every weekend."

"Where'd you live?"

"In South Braintree. It's a little outside. And one time when we were riding the T, we saw this guy who had his hair all spiked up with mousse or something. It looked like it could have been varnished it was so straight and . . ." Cassie pulled back and looked around but then leaned forward again. "And guess what was riding up there between the spikes on his hair?"

"What?"

"I don't know if I should tell you, you being a

country kid and all. I don't know if you could stand it."

"What . . . what . . . tell me." Cora grabbed her hat, her special Boston Celtics hat. "Tell me or else."

"Give it back." She grabbed for it, but Cora was too quick. "Okay, okay, I'll tell." She leaned close to Cora's ear. "It was a rat, a pet rat. He had a rat riding up there on his head."

"No."

"For real. Mom and I saw it. The guy got off at the stop at the park across from the State House. And then guess what?"

"What?"

"There was a picture in the paper the next week."

"Really?"

"Yeah, it showed the rat riding between the spikes of his hair."

"Cool."

"I know. It's fun living in the city. You see all kinds of cool things."

"Did you ever go to a Celtics game?"

"Well, no."

"How come?"

Cassie tried to think of a lie, but none came. If somebody else had asked her she could have said she didn't like the Celtics, but Cora was still holding her hat. She knew she was crazy about the Celtics. The truth found its way to her mouth. "It cost too much."

"Really? You couldn't go even a couple of times?"

"Well, Mom almost got these tickets cheap at work once, but it was a night game and we would've had to take the T home late at night, and — "

"But I thought you took the T all the time."

"We did, during the day. But Mom didn't like us to, at night."

"How come you didn't drive? We did, last year. Dad brought us in when they played the Bullets."

"We don't have a car."

"You don't?"

"No." Cassie looked down. She bent over and wrenched off a handful of long grasses and then pressed them into her fist.

"Not ever?"

"No, Mom's a secretary. I mean, she *was* a secretary. Secretaries don't make very much money."

"Oh . . . well . . ." Cora grabbed hold of the fence post and pulled herself up. She balanced on the lowest beam. Then she jumped down and plucked off a long piece of grass. She brought it to her mouth and blew across it.

It made a whining sound, a sound that Cassie didn't like. She shuddered.

Cora turned back to Cassie. "Well, you know, it doesn't matter. I mean, that's why your mom's going back to school, right? To better herself. My mother says it's really important for a person to better herself." Cora blew across the piece of grass once more. "I mean, I think it's great your mom's gone back to school."

Cassie rolled the grasses she was holding into a ball. She was glad that Cora thought Mom was doing something good. She almost felt proud of Mom for a second. But she certainly wasn't glad that she was at school. It was so confusing. She leaned on the fence post and looked down.

"You okay?"

"Yeah, just a little hot."

"C'mon, let's go to the house. We'll get some lemonade."

"Real lemonade?"

"Well, from a mix."

"With sugar and all the chemicals and everything?"

"Yeah, how else?" Cora was looking at her strangely, but then she stopped abruptly. "Oh, yeah, they don't let you have — "

It was so nice for somebody to know, without her having to tell them.

Cora grabbed her arm. "C'mon, we got a bag of Doritos, too. I'll race ya. Last one in has to open the bag."

Cassie started flying toward the farmhouse, the farmhouse that held the real mix lemonade with the real sugar and chemicals. She beat Cora by a good ten feet.

Chapter Nine

It was five o'clock, and the guests were due to arrive at six. Lots of Aunt Emily's friends from work were coming: Loretta, of course, and others that Cassie had only heard about.

"How many therapists will be there?" Cora had asked Cassie the night before on the phone.

"At least eight."

"Then you'd better keep your head covered."

"Cora, what are you talking about?"

"To keep it from being shrunk, you know, with all those shrinks being there."

"Ha, ha, ha."

Aunt Emily and Uncle Fred had spent the whole day in the kitchen making quiches and soups and breads, and other foods that Cassie didn't even recognize.

"Do you want me to chop something?" Cassie had asked, when she'd walked into the kitchen and seen Aunt Emily slicing piles of green peppers. Her mother had always taught her to offer to help when she saw someone doing a big job.

"No thanks," Aunt Emily had said, then turning to Uncle Fred. "I *told* you we should have made the Mexican casserole last week and frozen it."

"Calm down, Emily," he had answered. "We're fine, we have plenty of time. Unless the power goes off or something bizarre happens, we're fine."

"What do you mean, if the power goes off? Are they working on the line? Do you know something I don't?"

"Emily, look at me. The power is *not* going off. We're fine. It was just a stupid comment. I was trying to make a point. Now, *calm down!* This is supposed to be fun."

Cassie could see that she was in the way. Ernie came over for an hour or so in the morning and they played Monopoly, but he had to go to the dentist at ten-thirty. So she watched cartoons, even though it was hard to hear because Aunt Emily had the stereo blasting with classical music. It sounded almost as bad as Mr. G.

"Cassie, don't sit so close to that screen. It's not good for you," Aunt Emily said, walking through the living room carrying the punch bowl.

It's good for me to have my eardrums blasted out? Cassie thought, but she moved a few inches away from the TV.

Later, Cassie made herself a peanut butter and jelly sandwich, because they were too busy cooking fancy things to make her lunch. Then she took one piece of celery off the counter. Aunt Emily gave her such a dirty look that Cassie got out of there, fast.

She went for a walk, but that was boring, so she called Cora for a while until Aunt Emily asked her to get off the phone because guests might want to call for directions. Nobody did. Cassie knew, because she listened.

Then she called Cora back, about an hour later, and asked her to come over if she could get a ride. But Cora's parents weren't home, so Cassie thought that maybe Uncle Fred could drive her. But Uncle Fred said they were way too busy to drive Cora over. Aunt Emily reminded her that she'd asked her not to use the phone.

So Cassie hung out in her room, listening to her Walkman. Starting around three, she could hear them running around the house with the vacuum cleaner. Things were rattling and things were banging, so she stayed out of the way for a couple more hours.

She had just gone out to the kitchen to get a drink of water when it happened. The blue glass plate was on the counter arranged with cheeses and four different kinds of crackers, and radishes made into little flowers and Greek olives in the middle. Cassie loved Greek olives.

She was taking just one of the olives when her sleeve caught on the side of the dish and it dashed to the floor.

"Oh, no!" Aunt Emily was standing in the doorway. "OH, NO!"

"I'm sorry, Aunt Emily, I . . ."

"That was my *best* hand-blown plate. All that work, all that food, how *dare* you."

"I . . ."

"Get *out*, just get *out* of here."

Cassie turned to run, but Uncle Fred was standing in the doorway. "Emily, calm down, the child is more important than the darn plate."

"The child, I'm sick to death of the child."

Cassie wanted to run, but Uncle Fred was blocking the only exit.

Aunt Emily was still yelling, "We walk around on tiptoes, trying to make her happy."

"Emily, stop. This isn't right."

"Her mother's never taught her to do anything. She never does anything around here!"

Something exploded in Cassie. She heard herself screaming, "You don't *let* me do anything. Anything I do isn't good enough for you."

"That's not true."

"It *is*! You never let me do *anything*!" Suddenly, the words were roaring out of Cassie's mouth. "I hate you. I hate living here. I want to go home. I want my mother!"

Once she'd said it, there was silence in the room, silence that reached to the top of the ceiling. Uncle Fred moved toward her and, as he did, Cassie slid around his side and out the kitchen door.

She ran out into the yard and up the road, and was halfway up Wolf's Den Hill before she realized that she didn't have her jacket on. It was a cold October day. She shivered, but she kept on running.

I'm going the wrong way to hitch home, she thought, and then she remembered that she had no home to hitch to. Mom had given up their apartment because they couldn't afford to keep it.

Remembering their apartment made Cassie stop. It had been small, and their furniture had been old, but they'd gotten this great wicker couch at a tag sale and spray painted it white, and Mom had made big stuffed pillows out of wild Hawaiian print. They'd looked terrific in the living room.

Cassie realized she'd been running. She realized she was sweating. She was sweating and cold, and she was crying. With all her heart, she wanted her mother to be there.

"Maybe if I call her. Maybe, if I call her and beg her, and tell her how much I need her, maybe she'll come home!" Cassie knew it was only a hope. She knew that her mother wouldn't come back from Ohio.

Cassie looked around. She was almost to Brennar's farmhouse. The pasture with the five horses was up ahead beyond the maples. Cassie started moving again. She put her right foot down and then her left, and then it was natural to keep walking. She went past Brennar's and then took a right on the dirt road to the pond.

It was somewhere to go. It was familiar. No one would yell at her there. Besides, Cassie didn't have anywhere else to go.

Chapter Ten

She reached Puffett's ten minutes later. She'd stopped crying on the dirt road and thought she was finished. But when she saw the pond, the familiar cattails waving from the other side, the cedars shimmering in the wind, Cassie sat down on the big rock near the water and cried some more.

She cried differently now. She cried for all the old hurts, for all the days and nights she'd felt like crying but hadn't let herself, even for times she didn't exactly remember. She felt like she'd cry forever.

Then she heard a sound. She sat straight up. It was Ernie, suddenly there beside her.

How could she have been so stupid? Of course Ernie would come to the pond after he got home. He'd even told her he was getting home late this afternoon.

"Cassie — "

She buried her face in her hands and turned away. Why didn't he just go away! Why did he stay there!

"I'm sorry, Cassie. Are you okay?"

She couldn't stop sobbing. She felt she'd never stop crying, that all those tears would go on forever.

"Hey, look," Ernie said. "I cry lots of times. Hey, look, I'll go away for a while and then I'll come back to make sure you're okay."

He did. He walked through the marsh grass to the other side of the pond. After a while, Cassie could hear him plopping stones in the water. She stayed there, not knowing what to do.

Ernie came back. "If I had to leave my mom and dad, I'd cry, too," he said.

He knew. He just knew. That made Cassie cry harder for a while, but somehow she didn't feel as embarrassed. A gray squirrel came to the edge of the road and stared at them. The tears were lessening now, and staying more in her heart than going to her eyes.

"Well, I'm only leaving my mom," she heard herself saying.

"I know." He sat down near her, on the gravel. He drew circles on the earth.

"And you know what the worst part is?" Cassie said.

"What?"

"I don't even have a Kleenex, and I have a nose full of snot."

They both laughed, in spite of themselves. "I think I have one," Ernie said, as he reached in his pocket. He did have one, but it was pretty used. "You're going to have to do it the Indian way," he said.

"What do you mean?"

"Blow your nose in a leaf."

Cassie thought that was the most disgusting thing she'd ever heard of, but a nose full of crying was pretty disgusting, too, so she found a big oak leaf that had already fallen, and she blew her nose into it.

Sitting there with Ernie, blowing her nose in an oak leaf, Cassie began to feel better. The gray squirrel was still there, too, closer now, staring at them.

"I hate them. I want to go home."

"Call your mother."

"I can't. She'd get mad. She wants me to be nice to them. Besides, we don't even have a home."

"Oh."

They sat together in silence for a few moments, watching their squirrel jumping from brush pile to brush pile on the west side of the pond.

"Hey, Ernie."

"Yeah?"

"Will you . . . will you tell anybody?"

"Me? Are you kidding? They couldn't get it out of me." He stood up and hit his chest and made growling noises.

They were quiet for a while, a comfortable quiet. Then Cassie said, "It's weird being at school and like . . ."

"I know."

"I mean, I'm not mad at you at school or anything, but — "

"I know. Me neither." He finally just said it. "But sixth-graders and fourth-graders aren't supposed to be friends. It's like the law or something."

"Yeah." She picked up another leaf and blew her nose again.

"But maybe we could just keep it a secret, like we could be friends here but not at school."

Cassie shook her head. "Mom says secrets aren't good. She says they always catch up with you."

Ernie threw the pebble he was holding into the woods. He threw it hard, then picked up another and threw that. "She's not here, so what does she know?"

"How come you're mad?"

He sat down and hugged his knees. "I don't know. I'm not."

Cassie wiped her eyes. "Well, maybe that's what we should do. It's not like it's a bad secret or something." She looked directly at him. "We can have like a secret club, the two of us."

"You sure?"

"Yeah. Then we don't have to worry about what the kids say."

"You want to have a sign or something at school? Like a code?"

"Naw, let's just go undercover and pretend we don't know each other."

"It'll be like we're on a secret mission."

"To discover the horrible secrets of Northwood Elementary School."

"Agent Cassie Hannely and Agent Ernie Bartos on the case."

They laughed.

"You feel like skipping stones?" Cassie asked.

Ernie looked at his watch. "I can't. I gotta get back. Mom said to be back at six for supper."

Cassie watched as Ernie walked down the path to the road, and pretty soon she couldn't even hear his footsteps. She was so glad it was Ernie who had discovered her and not Cora. She liked Cora and everything, but Cora would want to tell everybody at school.

Having Ernie be her friend was like . . . she finally just said it straight out. Having Ernie be her friend was like having a little brother. If Dad hadn't died when he did, she might have had a little brother or little sister of her own.

Cassie knew she had to go back to the house. The early autumn light was already becoming less intense, and the sky was turning a light pink near the horizon. It was becoming nighttime already in those cold, unforgiving hills.

Sitting by the pond by herself, Cassie shivered. She knew that she had to go back. She was old enough to know that it wouldn't do her any good to catch pneumonia.

There already were unfamiliar cars in the driveway, and Aunt Emily and Uncle Fred both had tight looks on their faces when she walked in. Loretta waved hi from the pantry.

"Oh, this is your sweet little niece," one of the

new people said. She was a tall woman wearing flowered loose pants and an oversized tunic.

"Oh, she's so *cute*," said another. This one had on normal clothes, but a red scarf hung from around her long ponytail.

"So, Cassie, how do you like living in the woods?" asked scarf lady.

Cassie started to shrug, but flower pants interrupted. "Oh, I'm sure she loves it, all this healthy air. It's *so* good for a child. Don't you just *adore* it, darling?"

This time, Cassie got in half a shrug before Aunt Emily's voice was saying, "Cassie's got to get out of those dirty clothes and into the shower. Come on out for some supper, dear, when you're finished."

Later, in the shower, Cassie realized two things. It was the first time Aunt Emily had just plain out told her to do anything. It was also the first time she'd ever called her dear.

Cassie had just finished getting dressed when she heard a knock on the door. She was standing next to her Larry Bird poster, looking out the window.

"May I come in?" It was Aunt Emily. "Cassie, we have to have a talk."

"Okay."

Aunt Emily came in and sat on her bed. "I'm sorry, Cassie, I shouldn't have yelled at you. Uncle Fred was right. You're much more important to me than the stupid plate. I was just upset and I . . ." She stopped, holding her breath, but then she went on quickly. "I have been so worried about you. I know you didn't want to live with us. I know . . . and then when you wouldn't write your mother, I — "

Cassie didn't know what to do. She'd never had an adult, at least an adult other than her mom, apologize to her before.

Aunt Emily was still talking. "It's just that, all right, I'm just going to say it. I haven't known how to help you. I know you're upset. I don't blame you, I'd be, too. But, I don't know a lot about kids, and . . ." She sighed, "I guess we're just stuck with each other for a while and we're going to have to make the best of it." She reached over and smoothed the quilt, placing the teddy comfortably on top of it. "I mean, we wanted you. We wanted to have you here, but that's really different than what happened to you, because we had a choice."

Cassie held her breath even harder. Aunt Emily was right. They'd had a choice. Mom had had a choice. But not her. She kept staring out the window, as if there were a fascinating circus out there instead of only the trees starting to be hidden in the autumn evening.

"Cassie." There was a new tone now in Aunt Emily's voice. "You don't have to come out if you don't want to. There's a lot of people you don't know at the party, but, look. You want me to bring you a plate?"

Cassie shrugged.

"Or would you rather come out yourself and get something? Then you can at least have a choice about what you get to eat tonight." Aunt Emily almost chuckled. "What would you like?"

Aunt Emily had talked a lot. Cassie figured she had to say something. "Well, do I have to talk to anybody?"

Aunt Emily laughed this time. "I will personally escort you and keep every strange person away from you. C'mon, let's get you something to eat."

Aunt Emily did go with her, and she did intercept scarf lady who started to come over. And Aunt Emily didn't even say anything when Cassie chose only cheese and crackers and carrot cake for supper.

Uncle Fred brought the big radio into her room and stopped by a few times in the evening to see how she was doing. Cassie was very tired that night. She fell asleep by nine o'clock.

Chapter Eleven

When they stopped by at Mrs. Parnelli's the following Wednesday to get her list, she came out after the first honk, and easily climbed the stairs of the bus.

"Well, good morning," she'd said, "it's so sweet of you to do this for me."

Cora poked Cassie. "See, I *told* you she got nice."

Cassie poked Cora back. "I didn't say she didn't."

"But you didn't believe me."

Cassie shrugged. She'd have to remember to ask Ernie about Mrs. Parnelli later.

"Hey, Cora."

"Hey, what?"

"You gotta help me figure out what to get Aunt Emily for her birthday."

Cora giggled. "You could get her a milk purifier."

"Oh, sick. No . . . I could get her a . . . food chewer!"

"Gross!"

"No hey, it'd be great. Then she wouldn't have to chew so much. Think of how it would save wear and tear on her teeth." Cassie laughed. She couldn't stop herself. "And . . . and . . . it could be this little round thing that you put the food into. It could have its own set of teeth and . . . and . . ." She couldn't go on. If she hadn't been on the bus, she'd have been rolling on the floor.

Cora finished for her. "And when it's done chewing, it'll burp twice and spit the food into your mouth."

"Oh, gross!" But they both couldn't stop laughing.

Mr. G actually looked around to see who was making the racket. When he saw it was Cassie and Cora, he touched his hand to the brim of his hat, turned back around and started the bus.

By the time they got to Route 37, Cassie wiped her eyes and said to Cora. "You know what I think I'm gonna get her?"

"What?"

"That tie-dyed scarf we saw at Cartell's last week."

"But that was eight dollars."

"I know, I got money saved from last summer, when I took care of Mrs. Lasarian's dog. That's the kind of thing Aunt Emily likes, scarves like that."

"Pretty nice present."

"I know."

During creative writing, Mrs. Kalish asked Cassie to come to her desk. Her story about the rhino in the bathtub was sitting there.

"Remember this story? You wrote it a couple of weeks ago. I've liked a lot of the things you've written, Cassie, but I've got to admit, this is my favorite."

"It is?"

"Yes."

"But I think I messed up on some of the commas."

"You did pretty well." She picked up Cassie's story and held it. "Have you ever written stories before?"

"No, just stuff like what I did on summer vacation and things like that."

Mrs. Kalish laughed. "Pretty awful, huh?"

Cassie laughed, too. Mrs. Kalish seemed so different when she talked to her alone.

"Do you want to keep working on this one? You don't have to, but I think this one's very good." Mrs. Kalish handed Cassie her paper.

"I don't know."

"Well, you could have the rhino say something really outrageous, like, 'What are we having for dinner?' "

Cassie laughed, "Or he could want me to take him to school or something."

"That'd be fun. Do you think you can get started?"

Cassie nodded and went back to her desk. The kids were all working, quietly. After a while, she'd written:

The rhino blew more soap bubbles at me. "Cut it out," I said.

"What's your problem? I'm just trying to be cute and cuddly," he answered.

That didn't make any sense at all. "There's no way a rhino can be cuddly. And, besides, I don't want you to be cuddly. I want you out of my bathtub. I want you, in fact, out of my house!"

He looked hurt. "Does this mean you're rejecting me as your house rhino?" he asked, tears welling in his eyes.

"What?" I screamed. This was too much. "You want to be a house rhino? You're probably not . . . you're probably not even . . . house trained."

"I most certainly am," he said, and this time, he stamped his foot, and lots of water flew out of the tub onto the bathroom floor.

"Great," I said, "now I'll get in trouble again for the mess. It was pretty hard the last time, you know, explaining why the living room wall was all busted."

Cassie was interrupted by Mrs. Kalish telling them it was peer conference time. For the second time, Cora grabbed Cassie's paper.

"Cut it out," Cassie said. She tried to get her paper back, but Cora had moved her seat and was already reading it to a bunch of kids. This time, four or five kids were listening.

Cassie tried to grab it again, but then the kids were laughing, and she didn't know what to do.

"It's pretty funny, about the house trained part," Anthony said.

"Can you imagine how big his litter box would have to be?" said Cora.

"Oh, gross!"

Everybody laughed a lot, this time.

"I didn't know if I should put that part in," Cassie said. "Maybe Mrs. Kalish will get mad."

"No, she just doesn't like violence and stuff, blood and gore, things like that," Sarah told her.

"Last year," Margy said, "my sister wrote this thing about how her parrot did you-know-what all over the house. Mom and Dad always got mad, but my sister got what she deserved in the end."

"What?"

"Her sweet, precious parrot did it on her birthday cake!"

Everybody laughed.

"And she wrote about it?"

"Yeah, Mrs. Kalish said she probably learned a good lesson."

The bell rang for gym just then and, even though Cassie didn't like gym, it didn't seem as hard this time. At Northwood, they didn't always have to play baseball, like in her old school. Cassie hated baseball. She never could hit the ball. Whenever she was up at bat, she just wanted it to be over.

At Northwood, they did different things. That Wednesday, everybody got around a big parachute that was on the floor and picked it up. Mr. Wotysiak threw a ball into the center, and everybody tried to get it to bounce as high as they could. Mr. Wotysiak said they did it as well as any class he'd ever seen.

The grocery bags were piled up around Mr. G again, ready to be taken to Mrs. Parnelli on the way home that afternoon. Cassie and Cora both took huge steps around the bags, and when Cassie was halfway down the aisle, she heard Ernie asking Mr. G if he could help carry them in when they got there.

One strange thing had happened, though, as they were driving out of the school yard. As Mr. G was driving around the big circle, Mrs. Blanchette, the principal, had come out the side door and had motioned to him to stop the bus.

"Mr. G," Anthony had said, "Mrs. Blanchette wants to talk to you."

Usually, Mr. G heard what people said to him, even if they were in the back of the bus, like Anthony was. In fact, Cassie thought it was pretty good, how Mr. G could usually hear, even when the rest of the kids were talking or laughing.

But that afternoon, Mr. G didn't seem to notice Anthony at all. He just kept driving, and then started singing another aria, loudly this time, as soon as he turned onto Route 37.

"She's new," Cora said. "My mother says she's never been a principal before."

"How does your mother know?"

"She was on the search committee. My mother says she's from the city."

"Like me."

"Yeah, but you're learning the rules."

"What rules?"

"The country rules."

"Whaddaya mean?"

"Well, like she'd probably get mad if she found out about Mr. G getting Mrs. Parnelli her groceries. She'd probably say something about it not being 'appropriate' or something stupid like that. That's why Mr. G didn't stop. He didn't want her to see the bags."

"Oh."

"My mother says we just shouldn't say anything about it at school. My mother says that what Mrs. Blanchette doesn't know won't hurt her."

Cassie was surprised, but Cora was still talking.

"And my mother knows all about this stuff because she's from the city, too."

Cassie looked at her quickly. "She is?"

"Yeah, from Boston, just like you, but when she married my dad she moved out here. She says it's much better out here, a more wholesome environment to raise children."

"Not if you're teaching 'em to lie," Cassie said under her breath.

"What?"

"Nothing, I wasn't saying nothing."

When they got to Mrs. Parnelli's, she was looking out the window. As soon as she opened her kitchen door, she motioned to Mr. G to wait. She came out, carrying a big box.

"One for everybody," she said, after she'd climbed the stairs, "with a couple left over for the grown-up." She actually winked at Mr. G.

They were chocolate chip cookies. Better than that, they were huge chocolate chip cookies. Each one was worth at least three or four of the little ones. They were just like the ones Cassie's mom used to make on snowy winter Sundays.

"Great," Cora said. "I love 'em, but did you hear that Sarah can't eat chocolate anymore?"

"Why not?"

"She's got a zit, a genuine zit. Margy saw it and everything. Sarah's been trying to keep her bangs over her forehead so it won't show, but it'll never work. Margy *saw* it."

Cassie shrugged. She was happily eating her cookie and only half-listening to Cora.

"But you know that little kid, Ernie, in fourth grade?"

Cassie sat up.

"You know him, right?"

Cassie looked down.

"Margy said she saw a zit on his forehead, too. Isn't that weird, for a fourth-grader to have a zit?"

"What's Margy, the zit guardian of the school?" Cassie said, louder than she meant to. Nathaniel and

Anthony stopped talking and looked around at her.

"Why're you mad?" Cora asked.

"I'm not mad. I just want to eat my cookie without talking about zits."

When Cassie got back to Aunt Emily's and Uncle Fred's that afternoon, there was a letter waiting for her on the kitchen table. But she didn't open it right away. She waited until she'd taken out the trash and done all the dishes in the kitchen.

> *Dear Cassie,*
>
> *What is the problem? Why aren't you writing me? I'm calling this Saturday at 3, your time. Be there. I'm telling Aunt Emily and Uncle Fred, too.*
>
> *I'm sorry, Cassie, but I'm just upset, and I can't understand why you're doing this. Are you mad at me? If you're mad at me, tell me, and we can work it out.*
>
> *School is okay. I passed my first Chemistry test with a 68. I got 98 in Advanced Psychology of Aging.*
>
> *I'll talk to you Saturday. Be there.*
>
>
>
> *Love,*
> *Mom*
>
>

Chapter Twelve

As soon as Cassie heard the phone, she knew who it was. It was exactly 2:58. Cassie prayed that it was Loretta calling Aunt Emily, because Aunt Emily wouldn't be able to get rid of her for at least twenty minutes.

"Cassie," Aunt Emily called. "It's your mom."

Cassie thought about pretending she was in the bathroom, or that she had a fever, but she didn't have the energy to pull it off.

"Hi," she said, picking up the receiver. She was grateful that Aunt Emily left to go into the living room.

"How are you?" her mom was asking.

"Fine."

"Well, how's school?"

"Okay."

There was a long silence, and Cassie honestly tried to think of something to say.

"This is costing me money, you know," Mom said. She sounded mad.

Cassie didn't mean to be rude. "I didn't ask you to call."

"What's *happened* to you! You're not writing, and

I'm lonely here, too, and . . . I . . . I miss you, and it's driving me crazy. Are you crying?"

"No."

"You are, I can tell you are. Stop crying! I don't want you crying!" There was more silence, and then Mom said, "You didn't seem upset when I left. You seemed perfectly normal."

"It happened so fast."

"I told you in June. You had two months to talk to me about it."

"I didn't think you'd really do it. I thought you'd change your mind. I didn't think you'd really leave me."

"Honey, I'm sorry. Honey, please don't cry like that."

"You should have known. You should have just *known!*"

"Cassie — "

"Everybody leaves. You left, and Daddy left."

"Cassie, he died. It's not the same thing."

"What's the difference? He left. He should've been more careful. He . . ."

"Oh, Cassie, I wish I were there. I wish . . . oh, Cassie. I used to feel the same way. I used to be so mad at your dad because he died."

"You were?"

"For a long, long time. Maybe even until last year." Mom was silent for a moment. "Cassie, listen, I'll never leave you. I haven't left you. I am spend-ing nine months away from you so that I can give us a better life. I'm sick of being so poor. You wore that ratty old winter coat for three years and it made me feel bad every time you put it on."

"I didn't care. It was warm," Cassie said, even though she had minded last year when the kids had started making fun of her, calling her "Bigfoot gorilla coat."

"*I* minded. I want you to be able to go to college, and I want you to have nicer clothes, and . . ." Now her Mom was crying, too.

Cassie didn't know what to do. She still felt mad, and she didn't want to say she was sorry.

"I'm sorry, Cassie," her mom said. "I never wanted to hurt you. I thought it'd be nice for you to spend some time with Aunt Emily and Uncle Fred, get to know some family. We don't have any other family."

Cassie still didn't know what to say.

"Cassie, listen, there's not much use both of us crying on the phone. Listen, I love you. I'm going to be home at the end of May. Will you try? Will you please try to like living with Aunt Emily and Uncle Fred?"

Cassie didn't answer, but her mom didn't seem to notice, because she went on, "Okay, I have to go. I'll call again, soon."

Cassie heard the click of the receiver. She walked quietly back to her room. Aunt Emily was on the floor of the living room pinning up another quilt. She didn't seem to notice her as Cassie walked through.

Cassie lay on her bed, remembering those last few days at home, Mom had taken her shopping and had bought her a new pair of sneakers, new jeans, and a brand-new winter coat. It was just like what the other kids had. The label said PolarPlus, and it was green on the outside with a blue lining, with a collar you could turn up. When she'd told Mom it was too expensive, Mom had said that she didn't care how much it cost, that she should have spent the money last year. She said that this year, Cassie was going to have a nice winter coat.

How could Mom have known how much she hated that coat? She'd never complained. She'd never asked for another. She never would ask for something they couldn't afford. Lying on her bed, staring at her ceiling, Cassie just couldn't figure it out. How had Mom known about that old winter coat?

Half an hour later, Aunt Emily knocked on Cassie's door.

"Guess what?" she said. "I'm sick of cooking. We're going out for pizza, and . . ." She paused, as though something important was coming. "You can have any kind you want."

Cassie sat up, amazed. They'd never gone out for pizza before.

"Uncle Fred and I will share a large veggie, and

you can get a small pepperoni, or whatever you want."

"How about a hamburg and sausage?" Cassie asked.

Aunt Emily looked like she was going to throw up, but she swallowed and said, "Cassie, if you want a pizza with hamburg *and* sausage *and pepperoni* you can have it."

This was news. Cassie was truly amazed.

But there was more. Aunt Emily was still talking. "I know it's hard for you to eat our food. It must be really hard for you because you're not used to it, and you don't ever get what you like for supper."

Cassie looked up. She didn't know what to say.

"So Uncle Fred and I figured that maybe we could go out for pizza once a week, and then we could cook something for you special, like I could make a meat loaf and freeze it, or some of that special lasagna your mom sent us the recipe for. And then you could have it when we have something really weird."

"Like tofu with garlic sauce?"

Aunt Emily laughed. "Like tofu with garlic sauce."

Cassie said, quietly this time, "I'd like that."

"I used to make a mean meat loaf when I cooked with meat. I can probably remember how to do it."

Cassie wasn't all that hungry at supper because she was feeling tired, but she did order a pizza and she finished half of it. She didn't talk but, for once,

Aunt Emily and Uncle Fred didn't seem to mind. At least, they didn't bug her about it.

They gave her two dollars of quarters to play the juke box, and she got to hear lots of her favorite songs. On the way home, she told them about some of the rock groups she liked. That night, Cassie almost had a nice time.

Chapter Thirteen

Cora and Cassie were in the library getting books for their Irish immigration project. They were sitting on the floor in the corner behind the big divider, looking through the encyclopedias, when Ernie and Mr. Varella, the special-reading teacher, walked in.

"I'll help you find something," Mr. Varella said.

"I don't like these books."

"You don't like books, period . . . yet. C'mon, c'mover here." He went over to the picture book section and pulled a book out of the shelf. "Look at this one. It's a tall tale, *Paul Bunyan*."

"It's a picture book."

"It's okay, the drawings are very sophisticated. Look at the details here. Look, Ernie, you can use it to study for your drawings."

"Whaddaya mean?" He took the book and opened it.

"Well, you like to draw, and you're really good at it. I've seen your work. You should look at other artists, study them."

"But it's a picture book. I'm not going to read a picture book."

Mr. Varella sat down at the table in the center of the library. "It bothers you that much? We can keep it in the room, you don't have to take it back to class."

Ernie handed him back the *Paul Bunyan* book.

"Okay, how about one of the books over here?" He walked over to the Easy Reader section.

"I dunno."

"C'mon, you gotta choose something, and I know you can read these." .

"Kind of."

"How about this? This is actually a pretty good story. It's a classic."

Cassie leaned out past the divider a little and saw Mr. Varella give Ernie a book. Then she leaned back, fast, because she thought he might have seen her. Cora leaned out, also, farther than her, and Cassie grabbed her and pulled her back. Cassie put her finger to her mouth to silence her.

Mr. Varella and Ernie hadn't seen them. They were still talking.

"Okay," Ernie was saying, "if I have to."

"I guess it's come down to that," Mr. Varella said, "at least for today. But I haven't given up on you. You're a pretty smart kid and I'll get you reading yet." He picked up the *National Geographic* on the table and tapped Ernie lightly on the head with it.

Ernie didn't answer, but he followed close behind as Mr. Varella went back to class.

"Did you see. Did you *see*?" Cora asked when they were gone. "He had *Frog and Toad*!"

"So what?"

"That's for babies, for little kids."

"Hey, maybe he likes animals. Is that a crime?"

"Yeah, but if he's reading *Frog and Toad* in fourth grade, he must be pretty dumb."

Cassie forgot that she'd promised Ernie not to tell about their friendship. "He's not dumb! He's one of the smartest people I know!" Cassie put back the encyclopedia she was looking at, shoving it into its waiting slot. She got up.

"So what's your problem?" Cora asked. She was holding her encyclopedia close to her body.

Something about the way she said it made Cassie stop. Cora looked nervous, scared even, and all of a sudden Cassie didn't feel mad at her anymore. She sat down, leaning against the big *Atlas*.

"I like him, that's all. He's a nice kid. So what if he can't read too good. That doesn't make him stupid."

"Well," Cora said, "he *is* only in fourth grade."

"Yeah."

They looked through the encyclopedias for a few more minutes and then went over to the history section. They found a great book on Ireland that had a whole chapter on Irish immigration to the

United States. Mrs. Kalish loved it. She said that it was going to help them a lot with their report.

Aunt Emily had stayed home with a cold that day and was sitting at the table with her bathrobe on when Cassie walked into the kitchen after school.

"Hi, Cassie," she said. "Want some juice?"

"Yes, please. But I'll get it." She went over to the refrigerator and got out the Apple Cherry. "Want some?"

"Sure, I'd love it."

"Aunt Emily?" Cassie asked, giving her the juice and sitting down at the table.

"What, dear?"

"Can you like somebody . . . I mean, can somebody be your friend if they're not your age?"

"You mean, like Ernie?"

Cassie looked up. How did she know? She took a sip of her juice. Since she already knew . . . "He's only nine. He's a little kid. I'm in sixth grade and . . . Cora's supposed to be my best friend."

"Why do you like him?"

Cassie didn't expect a question. She put down her glass. "I don't know. He's nice, and we do fun stuff together, and . . . I don't worry about making mistakes when I'm around him."

"Sounds like a nice friendship to me."

"But he's a boy."

"So what?"

"Well, I guess if he was a fifth-grade boy or my

age, we couldn't be friends, but he's like my little brother." She got up from the table and looked out the window. "But Cora's supposed to be my best friend."

"Do you like Cora?"

"Yeah."

"Why?"

"She's nice, too, most of the time, and she's my age, and we go out to recess together."

"Sounds like there's a but in there, somewhere."

Cassie rested her head on the windowpane. "Sometimes she says awful stuff about people."

"You should tell her that you don't like it when she does that."

"Really?"

"It's hard, but if you really want a friendship with her, that's one of the best ways to start."

"Why?" Cassie asked.

"Because you've got to have honesty in a friendship."

It seemed impossible. Cassie didn't think she could ever tell Cora how she felt. "Aunt Emily?"

"Yes, dear?"

"Ernie can't read. I mean, he can read a little, but not real good."

"I know that."

"You do? How?"

"Well, I've known his family for a long time. Sometimes, during the week, his mom and I go to lunch together."

Dear Mom,

*I'm having loads of fun. We went tobag-
goning yesterday. I thought I'd hate it, but
I didn't. It's fun whizzing down hills at 80
miles an hour, and as long as everybody
remembers to veer far left, we don't even
crash into the dead elm anymore. Just jok-
ing. Ha, ha, ha.*

Love and kisses,
Cassie

This one was harder to throw away. She read it
and then read it again. Something was wrong. She
left it under her math book on the bureau.

Chapter Fourteen

Ernie didn't live on a real farm, either. Ernie's house was up past Cassie's, farther up the mountain and then off on a dirt road to the right. According to Cora's father, it was where it was supposed to be, not taking up valuable farmland in the valley.

The house was of modern design, with big thermopane windows to the south. Uncle Fred couldn't complain about the siting of Ernie's house.

The front door opened onto some steps. At the top hung an immense hooked rug that Ernie's mom had made. It had beautiful colors: deep purples and blues and greens. Cassie loved it.

And in the living room grew a tree, a real tree, right inside. Ernie said that it was a Norfolk Island Pine somebody had given them when he'd been born.

Ernie didn't have any brothers or sisters. His dad was an oil painter, but he drove a truck for a living. His mom was a secretary for Atkins Insurance.

On the day after Thanksgiving, Cassie and Ernie were sitting in the living room, playing Connect Four. Both Aunt Emily and Uncle Fred were working. Cassie was glad to be over at Ernie's, because she was still a little afraid to be in the house alone.

"Did your aunt and uncle make a turkey?" Ernie asked.

"A little one, for me, with walnut stuffing." It was nice of them to have done that. But yesterday, on Thanksgiving Day, Cassie *had* missed her mom and, also, her dad. It was a new feeling, missing him. Then, somehow, Cassie was saying, "My father wasn't a bum or anything. He just died."

"Oh."

"You think I'm lying."

"No."

"People always think I'm lying. They think my father abandoned us or something. But he died. He just died. I remember him and everything, from when I was little."

"Wow. I've never known anybody whose father just died."

"No?"

"No. I mean, how did it happen? Was he in a car wreck?"

"Kind of. A tractor fell on him."

"But I thought you were from the city."

"We are, now. After my dad died, Mom said she'd never live in the country ever again."

"Oh."

They sat, staring out the window, watching the snow collecting on the woodpile.

* * *

Cassie knew that Aunt Emily and her mom hadn't been close as kids. Aunt Emily was three years older, and when Mom was still playing with dolls, Aunt Emily was starting an underground junior high newspaper. She was always the rabble-rouser. It was odd because, of the two of them, it was Cassie's mom who finally got in more trouble.

For all of Aunt Emily's fighting for no dress code in high school and demonstrating against the Vietnam War in college, she graduated, got her job at the Clinic, and married Uncle Fred. Mom had quietly dropped out of college to marry Cassie's father.

"He was such a wonderful man," she always told Cassie. "He'd be so proud of you."

They'd come back to Ashford, where Cassie's dad had started a little business, a sawmill. They'd lived happily. They'd lived happily until that horrible day in April, when Cassie's dad was clearing some land and the tractor fell over him.

Cassie was three. She only remembered standing outside the living room, looking in at all the people sitting quietly, ever so quietly. She also remembered her mother, holding her tightly and crying, crying for hours, it seemed, until Aunt Emily came and pried her away.

That was Cassie's first memory of Aunt Emily. It was one of her few memories of her because, soon after, her mother sold the business and moved to the city. Aunt Emily and Uncle Fred had visited a few times, but Cassie sensed her mother's shyness with them, and she'd reacted the same way.

Grandma and Grandpa used to come up from Florida for Christmas, and they'd all see each other then. But since Grandma and Grandpa had died, within a year of one another, Cassie and her mom spent Christmas alone. Mom always said that it was a long trip up to Ashford.

They didn't get much money from the sawmill, it had so many debts. The money helped them that first year but, after that, Cassie's mom had to go to work.

She'd gotten a job as a secretary for an insurance company. The company paid for her to take college courses if she got at least a B, so every semester she took a course. She wanted to work with elderly people.

Cassie wanted her to become an important business executive, so she'd make lots of money and they could buy color TVs and VCRs and a velvet couch for the living room. But Cassie's mom wanted to get a degree in psychology and help elderly people, so that was that.

A few months before Mom had made her decision to finish school, full time, a strange thing had happened. Aunt Emily had come up and spent the day. She and Cassie's mom went off on a Saturday and spent the day together, all by themselves.

"What'd you talk about, Mom?" Cassie had asked.

"Important things."

"But what?"

"I'll tell you later. I've got a lot on my mind."

A week later, she'd asked Cassie how she'd feel about living with Aunt Emily and Uncle Fred.

"A weekend would be okay," Cassie had answered.

One month later, Mom told Cassie that she was going to have to live with them for a year. "I can graduate in two semesters if I go out to the Ohio campus. They're going to give me scholarship money and everything."

"How come I can't go out there with you? I won't be any trouble."

"We just don't have the money. The only way I can do it is for me to get a room in somebody's house, and help them with household jobs for the rent."

"But we can get two rooms, and I can help with the jobs, too."

"It just won't work, Cassie. It's better this way."

Cassie thought that it wasn't fair, that a school year was forever. She didn't want to leave her home and go live with strangers.

And besides, it was one of the few things Mom had ever told her she *had* to do. They usually discussed things.

They'd come back to Cassie's to watch TV. That morning, Cassie had been amazed to discover that

Ernie's family didn't have one at all.

"Hey, you two," Uncle Fred yelled from the living room. He'd come home early that day. "You know how to play chess?"

"No."

"C'mon in here. I'm going to teach you."

Cassie stood in the doorway. "I don't like playing games."

"You know how to play any?"

"Checkers."

"We play Life and Monopoly," Ernie added.

"Well, get in here. Both of your horizons are about to be expanded."

Cassie came halfway into the room, trying to think of an excuse to get out of it.

"I got these chessmen at a junk shop in the city," Uncle Fred was saying. "They're hand carved. Look at the horse."

"It's pretty good, but — "

"No buts about it. C'mon, sit down with me, and I'll just teach you a few moves and, if you don't like it after a few minutes, you can go back and watch the boob tube."

"Okay."

"Ernie, you sit next to me here and, Cassie, you sit on my other side. Okay, look, the horse goes two up and one over, and this is the king, and he can go wherever he darn well likes one space at a time, and this is the queen, she goes like this. Try it."

They sat for an hour, Uncle Fred showing them all the pieces. They didn't play a game, they just moved the chessmen and, pretty soon, Cassie and Ernie were whizzing the pieces around the board like they'd been doing it for years.

"Hey, you two are good," Uncle Fred said.

"We haven't done anything yet."

"You're learning the moves real fast."

"We are?"

"Yeah, faster than a lot of other people I've taught."

"Really?"

"Yes."

"Does Aunt Emily play?"

"No, she hates chess."

"Oh." Cassie suddenly felt uncomfortable, sitting so close to Uncle Fred on the couch. She shifted her weight and moved away from him a little.

"I think you're going to like it," Uncle Fred was saying. "I can tell. Tomorrow, we'll play your first game. I'll take you both on."

"I can't," Cassie said.

"I'll help. I'll be your advisor for your first game, but then . . ."

"What?"

"I'll show no mercy. As soon as you know what you're doing, it'll be war, real war."

"You'd better watch out," Ernie said.

"Oh, yeah, we'll see. I'll have no sympathy, no

sympathy whatsoever." Uncle Fred was scowling, and his eyes were slits. "There will be no sympathy from the Chess Demon of Fox Den Road."

Cassie laughed, and she didn't move away when Uncle Fred turned and tousled her hair.

Chapter Fifteen

"**D**id you hear?" Cora asked, as Cassie slid into her seat on the bus.

Cassie felt sleepy still, because Aunt Emily had woken her up a half hour late, and she hadn't had time to really wake up.

"Did you *hear*?" Cora demanded.

"Hear what?"

"Nathaniel asked Anthony to ask Sarah if she likes him."

"Likes who?"

"Nathaniel!"

"Why didn't he ask her himself?"

"Be real. So Sarah said that she thought he was cute but, all along, she meant Anthony because she's got a crush on Anthony, and she thought he was just pretending to be asking for someone else."

"Cora."

"What?"

"This is stupid."

"But everybody's talking about it."

"How did everybody find out?"

"Margy. She heard the whole thing."

Cassie closed her eyes and tried not to hear Mr. G singing at the top of his lungs. He'd been getting louder lately. Just then, there was a noise that none of them could ignore. "What was that?" she asked, sitting up straight in her seat. After last week's bus incident, when the brakes had failed, loud noises made Cassie nervous.

"Don't worry, it's just the hubcap again," Cora answered. "It always falls off."

"What do you mean?"

"This is bus C6, right? The hubcap always falls off."

"How come Mr. G isn't stopping?"

"He probably doesn't want to be late. Remember how mad Mrs. Blanchette got last week? He'll probably pick it up later, if he can find it."

Cassie stared at Cora for a moment, but then turned and looked out the window. After all this time, she was still being surprised by the strangeness. Was this the place she was supposed to call "home"?

Mrs. Kalish told them about their big writing project that morning. "It's time," she said. "It took us a while, but now I know that all of you can do it." She brought her chair to the front of the room and read to them.

First, she read *The Three Sillies*, a folk tale full of silly people doing ridiculous things. Then, she piled a bunch of fables and folk tales on the floor and let everybody read for twenty minutes.

"I can't do it," Cassie whispered to Cora, back at their seats, after she'd picked a book.

"Can't do what?"

"I can't do a project, and she says we have to read it to the little kids when it's done."

"I know. I don't like that part, either."

"Maybe I could get sick."

"Cassie, last year my sister's class worked on these for a month! You can't get sick for that long."

"I could try." Cassie tightened up the left side of her face, and her eyes seemed to bulge.

"Gross, how do you *do* that?" But Cora laughed.

"Practice, years of practice. One of the worst things about being an only child is that your mom always knows when you're faking being sick. I had to get really good . . . and not use it very much."

"Wow. But, Cassie, you write real good. You're better than me. I wish I could be as funny as you are when I write."

"But those were only little things. I can't write a story."

Mrs. Kalish was suddenly there, standing in front of their desks. But she didn't look mad. She had a book that she was holding out to Cassie.

"I wanted you to see this," she said. "It's a book of modern fables. It's got a story about a rhinoceros who goes to a store and sees this dress that's really fancy. She doesn't like it, but the saleslady tells her how nice she looks in it, so she buys it. The moral of the story is that flattery is a powerful force."

"But that's . . . silly, and rhinoceroses don't wear clothes."

"But that's the fun of it. In this kind of story, you can do whatever you want. In a way, they seem silly, but they really deal with very important issues in our lives."

"Oh." Cassie looked away.

"So," Mrs. Kalish said, "have you two decided what you're going to write about yet?"

"My sister wrote about why elephants have such big ears," Cora said.

"I remember, it was a great story."

"Can I do a retelling of *The Ugly Duckling*?" Cora asked.

"Sure, that'd be fine. How about you Cassie?"

"I don't want to retell an old one." Cassie was surprised to hear the words coming out of her mouth. And they were loud. She looked up at Mrs. Kalish to see if she was mad.

She didn't look mad.

"I want to write my own, but I don't know how to start."

Mrs. Kalish still didn't look mad, even though Cassie was talking to her just like she was a person, not a teacher. "Great," she answered, "you might try to just jot down a bunch of phrases, and it might give you an idea."

"Phrases?"

"Yes, you know, like thoughts, ideas, feelings. Just brainstorm, like . . . I bought Cleveland on Monday. Just jot down anything you can think of, don't worry if it makes any sense."

"Okay," Cassie said, as she got out her paper. She didn't think it would help, but at least it was something to do. She started to write:

I like reading. I hate math. Geography is for the birds. The sky is for the birds — hah, hah, get it?

Writing is disgusting. Mrs. Kalish is nice. Mr. G is nice, too, but weird.

She erased the whole last paragraph because Mrs. Kalish might want to see her brainstorm sheet. She started again.

Can pimples kill you? Girl crushed by a giant zit.

Then Cassie remembered the first writing assignment she'd ever had at Northwood, the one where Mrs. Kalish had told her to write about what she didn't do last summer. She started another paragraph:

I didn't go to the moon and eat bonbons. Actually, I hate bonbons. I didn't eat a

thousand pizzas. I didn't . . . I did . . . Do
your homework or die. Do this, do that, do
this, do that. Don't do this, don't do that.

All of a sudden, Cassie had an idea. She grabbed
another piece of paper and started to write.

Later that afternoon, when Cassie got back to the
house, she wrote her first letter to her mother:

> Dear Mom, in Ohio for a year,
> Aunt Emily's trying to make me meditate
> and become a Buddhist. Do you want me
> to become a Buddhist? She meditates in
> the living room, and she opens all the win-
> dows, wide, even when it's cold. She wants
> to commune with nature, she says.
> Uncle Fred says that if she wants to com-
> mune with nature, she should just go out-
> side, and Aunt Emily says that that's not
> the point, and Uncle Fred says well, then,
> what is the point, and Aunt Emily stormed
> out of the room. They're still not talking.
> That was Tuesday. They don't fight all the
> time. Just lots, lately.
> School's okay. I get to do anything I
> want.
> The brakes broke on the school bus last
> week while we were coming down Walnut
> Hill Road. Mr. G drove it into the pasture

at the bottom of the hill, and then he kept raving about how lucky we were to live in the country because if we'd been on a crowded city street, it would have been very dangerous. "Very dangerous," he kept saying.

Mr. G said that when the brakes were fixed over Thanksgiving, they should have done them right, and not used some cheap, rebuilt part that would break on the first hill.

"The town's too (blank) cheap," he said to Mrs. Blanchette — she's the principal. Anyway, "The town's too (blank) cheap to fix these brakes right, so cheap that they're willing to endanger the lives of their children to save a few measly bucks."

But then he told us later that he was just saying that part about endangering our lives to make a point. He said that he still had about ten percent of the brakes left when we were going down the hill. "Plenty," he said, "plenty to stop this old crate just fine."

Mr. G's cool. He let us look for the foxes' den in the woods while we were waiting for them to pick us up. We'd seen the baby foxes playing in the road the day before, the day that we'd stopped and watched them and Mrs. Blanchette got so mad at us

for being late to school. What was Mr. G
supposed to do? Run them over?
   I gotta run.

                        Your daughter,
                        Cassie

P.S. I'm still losing weight.
P.P.S. The hubcap fell off the bus this
morning.

She read it over. It was true, every bit, even the
losing weight part. At least, she thought that part was
true.

Cassie folded the letter into three equal parts and
sealed it in the envelope. She put it on the kitchen
table for Uncle Fred to mail.

When Cassie finished her letter, the pinkish light
of late afternoon was coming in the four big windows.
Cassie could see Uncle Fred out in the garden, dig-
ging up the last of the carrots. He'd asked her that
morning at breakfast if she'd help him put them in
the root cellar when they were ready.

"This is the latest I've ever left them in," he'd said.
"I'm afraid the ground will freeze, even with the hay
covering 'em that thick. I mean, we've already had
two snows, and Christmas is coming!"

Cassie ran out to the garden. There were piles of
carrots all around, and it was obviously too big a job
for one person. They spent two hours taking off the
tops and placing them carefully in brown containers,

putting first a layer of sand, and then a layer of carrots. When it had started getting really dark, they had turned on all the outside lights, and even Aunt Emily had come out to help.

"These are all the carrots we'll need for this winter," Uncle Fred said.

"Really? But won't they go bad?"

"Nope. That's why we have a root cellar."

Cassie had never seen so many carrots in her life. "Do they have bugs in them?" she asked, suddenly remembering the cabbage worms. Then she got scared that they might think she was rude, but Uncle Fred just laughed.

"Nope. These carrots are one hundred percent worm and bug and any kind of disgusting pest free. I personally guarantee it. Can't you see my stamp of approval?" He grabbed a carrot, wiped it with his shirt, and bit it. "See, here's my stamp of approval."

Cassie and Aunt Emily both laughed. "Pretty good," Cassie said. "Pretty good."

Chapter Sixteen

Cassie stood in the doorway of Ernie's room, looking at all his stuff.

He had models of race cars and airplanes, everywhere it seemed, even on the windowsills. There were pictures of animals tacked up on the walls, and dirty clothes and magazines were spread all around. Even Ernie's bed was covered with a raincoat and sweaters and a fishing pole.

"Don't your parents get mad?" she asked, climbing past the overturned chair in the middle of the floor, the chair that was leaning against the empty but dirty twenty-gallon fish tank.

"They used to, but my dad's as bad as me."

"Doesn't your *mother* get mad?"

"She's better now. We worked this deal that I keep my junk out of the *rest* of the house."

"Wow."

"Mom won't even come in here."

"She won't?"

"She says it's to protect her from getting ulcers."

"But how can you ever find anything?" Cassie asked, as she picked up a sneaker and grabbed the

Monopoly set that was half hidden under a plastic bag.

Ernie laughed. "I just keep throwing things around. Things turn up."

"Real efficient," Cassie said, but she laughed, too, as she threw him the set of dice that was nestled in a dried-up orange peel.

"Thanks."

"Beat you to the living room!" he yelled, as he grabbed the game from Cassie's hands and took off down the hall.

They set up the board on the rug in front of the fireplace. Cassie chose the wheelbarrow, as she always did, and Ernie picked his car.

Cassie already owned two railroads and a utility when Ernie's mom came in with a tray of milk and cookies.

"Thanks, Mom," Ernie said, as he reached for a fat chocolate chip.

"Does Cassie know about your birthday coming up next week?" she asked.

Ernie didn't answer. It seemed to Cassie that he turned a little pale.

Ernie's mom didn't seem to notice. She just kept talking. "You want a birthday party, honey?"

"No, Mom."

"But it'd be fun. Cassie could come over and you could ask some of the kids at school."

"Birthday parties are kid stuff," Ernie answered.

He was lying flat on his stomach, gripping the Monopoly dice in his fist.

"Well, we could at least have a cake and Cassie could come over, and we could — "

"I don't want a cake," Ernie said. "I don't *want* Cassie coming over." He threw the dice on the board so hard that they jumped and landed near the fire.

Cassie heard Ernie's mom saying, "You're being rude, Ernie. What's the matter with you?" Mostly, though, Cassie was feeling her face turning red. She thought that Ernie liked her, that he was her friend.

"I don't know why you'll never let us do anything for your birthday," Ernie's mom was saying. "Not for the last couple of years."

"I don't *want* anything, okay? I just don't *want* anything!" He jumped up and went over to the sliding glass door. He stood there, looking out at the forest.

Cassie got up to leave. If Ernie didn't want her to come over on his birthday, then he probably didn't want her visiting now. She grabbed her coat and gloves and headed out toward the porch. She didn't even say good-bye to Ernie's mother.

Ernie followed her out the side door and called to her as she reached the large maple. "Cassie!"

Something made her turn around, and Ernie ran to her and stood in front of her. "Cassie, I didn't mean now. I just don't want you coming over on my birthday."

"I don't get it. Are you mad at me?"

"No, it's not you. It's *me*. I hate my birthday."

"Did I do something wrong?"

"NO! I just don't want to see anybody on my birthday."

"Why?"

Ernie turned away. "I can't tell you."

"Why not?"

"I just can't tell you." His voice got softer, and then Cassie noticed there were tears in his eyes. He bent down suddenly and made a snowball and threw it deep into the woods.

Cassie looked down and kicked at the snow so that, in case Ernie was crying, he could wipe away his tears without her watching. She hated seeing him like this. When she finally looked up, she said, "You want to come over and see the new chess set Uncle Fred bought?"

"You mean it?"

"Maybe he'll give us another lesson."

Ernie ran back to the house and got his coat, and then they raced each other down the hill. Ernie was ahead for a while, but Cassie was out in front by the time they reached the curve near the white oaks. Cassie had longer legs. She always won their races in the end.

Cassie didn't think while she was running, but the thoughts came back as soon as they got in the house. All the time that she was showing Ernie the new chess set, all the time that Uncle Fred was showing them some new moves, Cassie kept thinking. Why does Ernie hate his birthday? How come he doesn't want a party? How come he doesn't even want me to come over by myself?

It didn't make any sense. It didn't make any sense at all.

Later that afternoon when Ernie had gone home, Cassie didn't think much about it when she heard the phone ring. Loretta often called Aunt Emily at that time. Uncle Fred called it their afternoon telephone fix. Sometimes, Uncle Fred was pretty funny.

And Cassie wasn't surprised that Aunt Emily was on the phone so long, because they usually talked at least half an hour. But she was surprised when, suddenly, Aunt Emily yelled, "Cassie, it's your mom. She wants to talk to you!"

She didn't know what to do. Was Mom mad at her again? She went slowly to the phone. "Mom?"

"Cassie, it's good to hear your voice."

"How come you called?"

"I was concerned about a few things you mentioned in your letter."

"What?"

"Oh, like the bus, and . . . nothing, dear. I feel much better now . . . now that I've talked to Aunt Emily. I'll write you about it."

Cassie stopped clutching the phone. It didn't sound like Mom was mad at her. "Hey, Mom."

"Hey, what?"

"I read the beginning of my story in sharing, and everybody clapped."

"What's sharing?"

"It's when you read to the whole class."

"Great. What's your story about?"

"It's a surprise, but it's a make-believe fairy tale. I'm making it up."

"Great. Will you send me a copy?"

"Okay, when it's done."

"Cassie, I called for another reason, too. I just want to tell you how bad I feel about not being there for Christmas."

Cassie couldn't say anything back. Suddenly, all she could remember was that old, sick feeling.

"I'd take the bus, but I can't be away from Mrs. Schneider for that long. When I took this job, I told them I'd stay for Christmas. It was one of the original deals we made, and I just can't back out. It's not right."

Even though she knew the answer, she still asked the question. "How come you can't fly out for a couple of days?" If Mom really cared, she would.

"If I had the money, if I even had some of the money, I would, sweetheart." She was quiet for a long time. Then she added in a soft voice, "I guess I didn't know how much it would bother me."

"But — "

"I'm so sorry, honey. This is so hard. . . ."

Was Mom going to cry? Cassie suddenly didn't

want that to happen, so she said, "Hey, Mom, you'll never guess what I'm getting you."

"What?"

"It's a surprise! I'll never tell! What're you getting me?"

"Hah, hah, you'll have to wait to find out, my dear." Mom's voice was louder now. "But, Cassie, I've got a surprise for you right now. I've decided that I'm going to call every Saturday, around suppertime."

"You are? Really? But, but, I thought we were poor."

Her mom laughed. "Well, we don't have tons of money, but we're going to talk every week."

Cassie didn't know what to say. "When are you going to call?"

"Saturdays, around six. Aunt Emily says you're always home."

"Every Saturday, you're going to call every Saturday?"

"At six."

Chapter Seventeen

Dear Cassie,

First, Aunt Emily says that she's not trying to make you become a Buddhist. She's not even a Buddhist. She just uses that style of meditation, and she only asked if you wanted to join her (in meditation) that one time.

Aunt Emily says that you do have lots of choices at school, but that's part of a very well-thought-out curriculum, and it probably just seems different to you because you always had to do things "their" way back at Westland. Aunt Emily says that Mrs. Kalish was very clear about the educational objectives at the Open House. It sounds good to me.

Aunt Emily says that she, too, was very concerned when you told her about your adventure on the bus. When she called the school, they told her that Mr. G did a masterful job of handling the situation, and that all the buses went through a thorough in-

spection before they let them back on the road. So I don't want you to worry any more about it.

What is this about you losing weight? Aunt Emily says that she knows nothing about it. I've asked her to weigh you, and she's going to buy a scale. What are you eating for breakfast? Are you having school lunch?

Things are fine here. I'm ignoring Mrs. Schneider who's insisting that butterscotch fudge has a trace ingredient that all elderly people need every day. I don't think she's an old person at all! I think she's a spoiled, selfish, bratty, obnoxious, stubborn, know-it-all, pesky three-year-old masquerading in an old person's body. This is really making me rethink my idea about working with elderly people when I graduate, except I keep reminding myself that there're all kinds!

Mrs. Schneider's daughter, Merilyn, visited last Sunday and told me that the person who stayed with her last year didn't even try to keep her diet in check. Once, Merilyn happened to visit at suppertime (uninvited and unexpected, of course) and found them both eating Doritos and lemon meringue pie. They tried to tell her that they'd already eaten.

But when Merilyn asked them, "Well, then, where are the supper dishes?" they had nothing to say. They tried to tell her that they'd ordered out for Chinese, but they couldn't produce the containers, either.

It's disgusting. Remember when I used to get so mad at you because all you wanted for supper was meat loaf and french fries? Well, Cassie, now I know that you were a breeze. I could actually get you to eat some things that were good for you.

I gotta run. I certainly do blab on in my letters. I'll talk to you Saturday (it feels so good to be able to say that).

Love and hugs,
Mom

P.S.

By the way, how come you can remember every little bit of what Mr. G says, when you had such a hard time learning your multiplication tables?"

Dear Mom,

Multiplication tables are boring.

I went over to Cora's last Saturday. She's my best friend. The snakes in the pantry didn't bother me that much, and Cora's dad said they probably weren't even poisonous. He told Cora's mom to just stop

*screaming and making such a fuss. He said
that if you lived on a farm, you had to learn
to coexist with a few little critters now and
then, and if Cora's mom wasn't such a city
girl . . .*

*I don't know how Cora could have
known what was going to happen but, as
soon as he said that, about her mom being
a city girl, Cora grabbed me real hard and
pulled me down on the floor under the
kitchen table. That's when her mom started
throwing plates. Cora told me that she
wasn't really throwing them at her dad, that
she was just throwing them around. I guess
Cora's mom doesn't like to be called a city
girl.*

Well, I gotta go.

*Your daughter,
Cassie Hannely*

*P.S.
How come Merilyn gets to boss Mrs.
Schneider around? Will I be able to boss
you around when you're old?*

Cassie knew that it was Ernie's birthday. She'd
gotten him a set of felt pens and a drawing pad with
one hundred sheets. She'd bought it with her own
money. Aunt Emily had given her some nice wrap-
ping paper with balloons and HAPPY BIRTHDAY
written all over it.

Cassie had gotten the present ready the night before. It was waiting on her bureau, waiting for the next time she'd see him alone, because she wouldn't go up to his house on his birthday.

Cora was over that Saturday morning. They were hanging out in her room when the phone rang.

"Cassie!" Aunt Emily yelled. "It's for you."

"It's not Mom, is it?" Cassie asked, taking the phone.

Aunt Emily shook her head no.

"Hello?"

"Hello, Cassie, this is Ernie's mom."

What was she doing, calling her? Was Ernie all right? She finally remembered to be polite. "Hello, Mrs. Bartos."

"I want to invite you up for some cake."

"When?" The question sounded rude, even though she hadn't meant it that way.

"Oh, in the next hour or so."

"But I can't."

"Why not? Your Aunt Emily says you're free."

"Well, Ernie . . ."

"Oh, he's just so shy. I really want to surprise him. I know he'll love it."

Cassie felt confused, but she still didn't think that Ernie would want her to come over. He'd asked her not to. "But Cora's here."

"Even better. Bring her up. It'll really be like a party. So . . ." She didn't wait for Cassie to say anything else. "I'll expect you by eleven. 'Bye." She hung up.

Cassie stood there, holding the phone, feeling terrible. "I can't," she said to Aunt Emily.

"His mom thinks he's just shy, Cassie. She wants him to overcome that. And you've gotten him such a nice present. Why don't you just bring it up? You don't have to stay long."

For a moment, Aunt Emily looked like Mom. But then she looked like herself again, and Cassie really wanted her mother. If her mother were there, she'd know what to do. If her mother were there, she could tell Cassie the right thing to do.

Ernie's mom let them in. "Oh, great!" she said. "I'll tell him you're here. Come on in."

Cassie didn't see it at first but, as they waited in the kitchen, she saw a gorgeous cake on the counter, standing tall with fluffy white frosting and covered with candles. Cassie frowned.

Mrs. Bartos came back into the kitchen. "Ernie let me make him a cake this year," she said, bringing in onto the table. "German chocolate with white chocolate frosting. It's so rich, you get fat just by looking at it."

"It looks beautiful, but . . ."

"But what?"

"It's got, it's got too many candles on it."

"No, it doesn't, it's got twelve. See, count them."

"But, I thought — " Cassie stopped. She felt confused. She suddenly remembered that Cora was with her in the kitchen. She didn't know exactly what was going on, but she was pretty sure that she didn't want Cora to know about it.

Ernie was suddenly standing there, staring at her, staring at all of them.

"I don't understand. What are you talking about, Cassie?" Mrs. Bartos was saying. "What did you think?"

Ernie answered for her. He answered so softly that they could barely hear. "She thought I was going to be ten, not twelve." He turned and walked quietly away, and there was silence in the kitchen.

"Cassie, why did you think Ernie was going to be ten?" Mrs. Bartos finally asked.

Cassie didn't really want to answer, especially with Cora standing right there. But Ernie's mom was looking at her closely, and Cassie knew that she was demanding the truth. "Because . . . because he's in fourth grade and he told me he was nine. And he's in fourth grade, and I just figured that, but, but maybe he didn't tell me and I just heard it wrong. I hope he doesn't get in trouble. Ernie never lies."

"It seems that he lied about this."

Cassie shrugged. She wished that she was somewhere far away.

"Ernie actually *told* you he was nine?" Mrs. Bartos asked.

"Yes," Cassie said.

Ernie's mom sat down at the kitchen table and started smoothing the frosting on the cake. She just kept sitting there, smoothing the frosting, not saying anything.

Cora hadn't said a word the whole time they'd been in the kitchen, but suddenly Cassie noticed that she was shuffling her feet. "Well, maybe we should go," Cassie said. "I'm sorry if we caused trouble."

"Oh, no, dear, you didn't cause any trouble. I'm glad I found out. I didn't think he felt so bad. I thought he was handling it well, but I guess, I guess I was wrong." Mrs. Bartos looked like she was going to start crying. Cassie was almost sure she was crying a little already.

Cora grabbed her by the arm, and they left by the kitchen door. As soon as they got in the yard, Cora started talking. "Wow! He's lied to *everybody*! He's lied about his age to *everybody*. This is gonna be great when I tell the kids."

Cassie stopped. She felt her body tense, and she stopped. "No," she said.

"What are you talking about?"

"If you tell one single person about this, I'll never speak to you again."

"What do you mean? He *lied*! He can't get away with that."

"So what if he lied. Haven't you ever done anything wrong?"

"Not like that."

"Gimme a break."

"I *haven't*."

"Yeah, I forgot. You're Little Miss Perfect."

Cora pressed her lips together and didn't say anything. She turned and started walking down the hill. After a minute Cassie followed, staying a few feet behind her the whole way down to the house.

Aunt Emily was in the kitchen making cookies. "You're staying for lunch, right?" she asked Cora.

"I gotta call my mom to come get me," Cora said.

Aunt Emily looked surprised. Cassie was glad.

All she could think of was Ernie standing in the kitchen, telling his mom about his lie. She dialed his number a couple of times, but then she hung up before anybody answered.

Cassie was lying on her bed, not even listening to her Walkman, when there was a knock on her door. Aunt Emily poked her head in. "Are you okay, honey?"

Cassie shrugged.

"You feel okay?" Aunt Emily started coming toward her, but stopped. Then she quickly walked over and put her hand on Cassie's forehead.

Cassie knew she shouldn't, but she pushed her hand away and sat up suddenly. "You shouldn't have told me to go!" She gasped.

Taking a backward step, Aunt Emily stayed there silent for a moment, but then she pulled up the chair by Cassie's bed and sat down. "You're right. I should have encouraged you to follow your instincts. You were right. I was wrong."

Such simple words, but Cassie started crying then, the tears beginning in her chest as a heavy feeling and then coming out lightly from her eyes. Aunt Emily got up and took the Kleenex box from the bedside table and put it next to Cassie. She didn't take one.

Aunt Emily started talking again. "His mom meant well, but she shouldn't have, we both shouldn't have meddled, especially me. You have such good instincts. I should have let you work this out with Ernie. I'm sorry, Cassie."

Cassie took a Kleenex and blew her nose.

"It's important for Ernie's mom and dad to know how he feels," Aunt Emily went on, "but I sure wish they'd found out some other way."

She was stroking Cassie's face by then, and Cassie didn't turn away. Then Aunt Emily said, "You can't do anything about it now. Except, you want to call him?"

Cassie shrugged. "No, I've already tried, but it doesn't seem right. I guess I'd rather talk to him in person."

"You sure? Maybe a phone call would be good." Aunt Emily laughed a little. "I'm doing it again, aren't I? Meddling." She got up. "Look, I'm going to make us some hot chocolate, and you come on in the kitchen when you're ready. We'll sample those cookies I just made."

"Cookies?"

"Chocolate chocolate chip. We'll get chocolated out." Aunt Emily laughed. "Maybe we'll even eat them all before Uncle Fred finishes bringing in the wood."

Cassie looked at her aunt. Was she serious?

"Aunt Emily?"

"What, Cassie?"

"How come . . . how come you eat cookies if you're into all that health food stuff?"

Aunt Emily laughed. "There're things that are more important than health food," she said. "Like being happy. I figure, for all that I lose by eating some junk, I gain in psychic energy."

Cassie looked at her, hard this time.

"You know what I did once?" Aunt Emily was saying.

"What?"

"I made a big batch of oatmeal cookies. They were so good that all the time I was making supper, I kept having just one. By the time supper was made, I was stuffed."

"Did you finish all the cookies?"

"You bet."

Cassie laughed. "Did you eat any supper?"

"Nope."

Sometimes, Aunt Emily acted like kids would act if only they could get away with it, thought Cassie. Sometimes, I like Aunt Emily a lot.

Chapter Eighteen

My dearest Cassie,

No, you don't have to write unless you want to. As long as I can talk to you once a week and know that you're all right, I'm fine. I do love getting your letters, though. I even love the funny ones, where you exaggerate a little.

Cassie, I promise you, I will never, never be like Mrs. Schneider when I'm old. If I am, you have my permission to show me this letter, and I'll immediately change my ways!

It's ridiculous. After I wouldn't give in to the butterscotch fudge ploy, she actually had this kid call me up, pretending to be her doctor. The kid (doctor) told me that she was supposed to be able to have anything she wanted, and my refusal to cooperate was causing her to have high blood pressure. High blood pressure, my eye!

So I called Merilyn and she said that the kid was probaby the paperboy.

So I confronted Mrs. Schneider, and she had a fit, a genuine screaming, yelling, stomping on the floor fit. She said that she was going to tell Merilyn that I was lazy and that I smoked (Merilyn hates anybody that smokes), but I told her that Merilyn would never buy it, and that she should just give up and get used to a healthy diet, at least while I was around.

And then she told me that I was fired, but I reminded her that Merilyn's always been the one who pays me and lets me stay. Thank goodness Merilyn told me last time that it's her house.

I don't know if it's worth it, Cassie. The thing is, I don't think it's the food at all. I think Mrs. Schneider enjoys the fighting.

How's school? I'm glad to hear about your story. Won't you give me any hints? I can't wait to read it.

Hugs and kisses and I gotta run,
Mom

Dear Mom,
The throwing up wasn't so bad, it was the . . .

It wasn't right. She made the basket in one shot. Two points!

Dear Mom,
I kept throwing up and we didn't have
any lights and . . .

No. The famous Larryetta Bird made a six-foot jumper!

Dear Mom,
We are pretty far from the hospital, but
Uncle Fred says he can get through any
snowstorm in the four-wheeler. He . . .

Cassie didn't even shoot this one. She crumpled it up and took it over and dropped it in the basket. She *had* been sick on Sunday. She had thrown up once, and Aunt Emily had put her to bed with the teddy and the panda bear from their room.

She'd felt better by noon, but they'd made her stay in bed because her temperature was still up. They'd heated up soup on the wood stove for lunch and, by late afternoon, when the electricity was still out, they'd set her up on the couch in the living room, next to the fire.

They had soup again for supper, and Aunt Emily and Uncle Fred had baked beans, but Cassie didn't because her stomach was still a little funny. They set up candles under the eaves outside of the sliding glass door, and watched the snow come to rest on the garden.

Cassie and Ernie stood in the school yard. Cassie stared back at the classrooms. Ernie seemed fascinated by the maples behind the swings. Cassie wished that she'd never gone over, that she'd never even seen him standing there, all by himself near the bushes.

She started kicking snow, and that made her suddenly mad, and suddenly she was mad at Ernie and saying to him, "How come you had to lie to me? I wouldn't've told anybody."

"You brought Cora over. Cora's got the biggest mouth in the school. You brought Cora over *on my birthday!*"

"I didn't mean to. Your mother — "

"I *told* you I didn't want you over on my birthday."

"I know. I'm sorry."

"Oh, sure."

"I *am*. I'm *SORRY!*"

"How could you do it? How could you come over when I asked you not to?"

Cassie didn't have an answer for that. She started kicking more snow at the bushes. "I'm sorry," she said. "I'm sorry, Ernie."

He was quiet, but when she apologized that last time, he looked at her.

"But how come you just didn't tell the truth?" Cassie asked. "What's the big deal that you're two years older?"

"You don't know what it's like, staying back. I've stayed back twice. The kids would make fun of me, if they knew."

"But you could've told me." Cassie looked away. All of a sudden, she thought that Ernie should have told her he was her age. If she'd known that Ernie was her age, she never would have let him see her cry, up by the pond that day in the fall. And how could she have a boy her own age as a friend? Maybe even a best friend?

"I wanted to tell you," he was saying. "I just got used to lying."

"Oh," Cassie said. She kicked some more snow. "But don't the teachers ever say anything?"

"I never lie in front of them, and they never say anything. I'm small. Everybody thinks I'm younger."

All of a sudden, Cassie laughed, without thinking. All of a sudden, it seemed pretty funny. "You got away with it for a long time."

Ernie smiled a little. "Yeah. I always wondered what I was going to say when I had to start shaving in sixth grade."

They laughed together then, and Cassie laughed so hard, her stomach started hurting again. "But, hey, Ernie, did your mother get mad?"

"No, worse than mad. She was crying."

"What did she say?"

"Oh, we had a talk. It was the 'Ernie, you're not stupid, you just learn differently than other people' talk. We've had it before."

"Oh." Cassie looked down at the ground again.

"She just kept saying I wasn't stupid."

"Well, you're not."

"Then how come I've stayed back twice?"

"I don't know. It doesn't matter."

"Yeah, right."

"But you always clobber me in Trivial Pursuit."

"You have to read all the questions."

"So?"

"I'm supposed to be in sixth grade, and I'm reading a third-grade book." He said it like it was the end of their talk.

Cassie grabbed some snow and made a snowball.

"You can't make snowballs," Ernie said. "School rule."

"I know the rules. I'm not dumb." She pressed the snow in her hand until it compacted into a little ball, and then she dropped it on the ground. Then, she felt bad that she'd used the word *dumb,* but Ernie didn't seem to have noticed. He was standing, looking away.

The duty teacher was ringing the bell just then, so they had to go in, but Cassie whispered as they were nearing the door, "Don't worry, I won't tell."

A look of gratitude crossed Ernie's face. "Really?"

he said, and then he paused. "But what about Cora? She's got the biggest mouth *in the school!*"

"I'll take care of Cora," Cassie said.

"But how can you?"

"Don't worry about it. I just will."

"You talk too much," Cassie said.

"Well, you write stupid stories," Cora answered.

"At least I don't write them about anybody real. I make up stuff."

"You think you're better than everybody else."

"I don't. At least, I don't make fun of other people."

A look of hurt crossed Cora's face, and Cassie was sorry that she'd said the last part. She tried to explain. "I mean, how come you always say bad things about people?"

"I don't say bad things about *you.*"

"Not to my face."

"What do you mean?"

"Well, if you talk about *everybody* else, I figure you talk about me behind my back."

"I *don't!*"

"Well, why do you bad-mouth people so much?"

"Nobody likes me, okay? I have a big nose." Once she'd said it, a look of surprise crossed Cora's face, and she said it again. "They don't like me. Nobody likes me." Cora looked like she was going to cry.

Cassie had gone too far to stop now. "Well, maybe

if you were nicer to people, they'd like you. It's got nothing to do with your nose."

"Yeah, sure."

"No, I mean it."

"And, how am I supposed to do that, Miss Popularity Plus?"

"Just shut up once in a while, just *shut up!*" If Cassie could have left, she would have. But Mrs. Kalish was depending on them to straighten up the library, so she was stuck. She went over to the picture book section and started putting the books that the little kids had dumped on the floor back on the shelves.

Cora was still sitting at the table, looking at her hands clasped on her lap.

On impulse, Cassie said, "I mean, you can be nice. You can be really nice. Remember the day we went Christmas shopping at the mall? You were just as nice as anybody. You were even as nice as Ernie."

"I was?"

"Yeah, you didn't make fun of anybody the whole day."

"Well, but remember we laughed at that lady with the mohawk with her hair all permed in the middle?"

"Yeah, but that was different. We were laughing at her hair. And she *made* it look weird like that."

"She *was* weird," Cora said.

"Yeah," said Cassie.

They sat in silence a few minutes more, and then

Cassie asked, "You think my stories are really stupid?"

"No, I just said that. I was mad."

"Oh."

"I mean, I wish I could make up stories like you can. All I can ever think about is other people's stories."

"Well, maybe you should write soap operas or something."

"Whaddaya mean?"

"You like to talk about other people all the time, and that's what they do in soap operas."

"Really?"

"Yeah."

Cora got up from the library table and went and picked up an alphabet book that was on the floor near the dinosaur section. She put it on top of the shelves near where Cassie was.

"Cora?"

"Yeah?"

"Do you think you could not tell anybody about Ernie?"

A pained look crossed Cora's face. "But it's such a good piece of gossip, it's going to kill me."

"Have you told anybody yet?"

"No," Cora said.

"Really? You haven't? You really haven't?"

"I haven't." Cora sighed.

"But why?"

Cora shrugged. "I don't know. I thought you'd be mad at me if I told."

Cassie was amazed. She took a few deep breaths before she asked Cora the next part. "Do you think you could keep it a secret? Only you and me and Ernie would know?" Cassie waited, holding her breath.

"I don't know," Cora said. "It's such a good story. I don't know if I can do it."

"Please, Cora. PLEASE! I'll help you write a soap if you don't tell."

"You don't have to."

"No, it'd be fun. You could come over next Saturday and we could work on it."

Cora sighed, a long sigh this time, but then she shook her head and giggled a bit and said, "Maybe I could sell it and make a ton of money and then I could get a nose job."

"I don't think your nose is that big."

"Are you kidding? It's huge. It's humongous. I could support an ant colony in this nose."

"Gross!" But Cassie laughed. She turned to look Cora in the eye. "You won't tell?"

"I won't tell, even though it may kill me."

"Gimme five," she said, and when Cora's hand met hers, the deal felt finished.

Chapter Nineteen

Dearest Cassie,

Only a minor crisis in the lab today. The beaker of hydrochloric acid was falling, but Rob (the assistant) made a flying leap and caught it two inches from the floor.

When he gave me a B for the day, I asked him how come, since I hadn't recorded the measurements right, either. He told me that he gave me a B for effort.

But I think he's just decided that he's got to pass me so I won't come back. I overheard him saying something about "dangerous to all of our safety and health." I certainly don't mind him giving me a false grade (especially if it's passing), but I do resent him telling other students about it! I do have some pride left, even if it's very minimal at this point in chemistry lab.

Mrs. Schneider is very quiet, and I'm worried. This isn't like her. She even ate the scalloped potatoes I made last night. Maybe it's working. Maybe with Merilyn

*sending us the menus for the week, maybe
she's given up fighting. Why don't I feel
better about this?*

Well, my darling, I'm off to the library.

*Tons of hugs,
Mom*

Dear Mom,

*Here's a copy of my story. Aunt Emily
typed it and xeroxed it at work. Uncle Fred
says he likes it. Mrs. Kalish is making me
read it to the third- and fourth-graders next
week. I told her I'll be so scared I'll throw
up, but she told me not to be silly. She's
still making me do it.*

*Your daughter,
Cassie*

*P.S. How come some kids can't read?
Even if they're smart?*

IN THE LAND OF DON'T
By Cassandra Hannely

Once upon a time in a land not very far from
here, lived a princess named Nicole. Now, Nicole wasn't your ordinary princess. She didn't
have long, flaxen hair, and she wasn't very
pretty, and she didn't get everything she
wanted.

In fact, Nicole hardly ever got anything she wanted, for she lived, you see, in the Land of Don't.

''Don't have any ice cream,'' said her mother, the Queen. ''It'll spoil your supper.''

''Don't watch TV, your homework's not done,'' her father, the King said.

''Princesses aren't supposed to have homework,'' said Nicole. ''And, besides, all I ever hear around here is don't, don't, don't!''

''That's natural, my dear,'' said her parents, in perfect unison. ''For you see, we live in the Land of Don't.''

With that, our princess stamped her royal feet and marched out into the garden.

She was desperate. It was easy to tell she was desperate, for what she did next was go frog hunting in the pond. She found a big, fat, juicy one. ''Yuck,'' she said, ''I can't do it, I just can't do it.'' But then, she thought of entering her teenage years, living alone with her parents in the Land of Don't.

Our brave, plucky princess puckered up her lips and landed a big fat, juicy kiss on the head of the frog. It slimed out of her hands and jumped back into the pond.

''Now I'm mad,'' Nicole announced, as she grabbed the first frog she could see: a skinny, almost emaciated, yellowish looking one.

''This is ridiculous! You're not going to turn into anything. You're even pathetic as a frog!'' But she kissed it.

Lightning clapped. Thunder roared.

''Don't stay out in the garden, it's going to rain,'' shouted her parents from the living room. Again, they were speaking in unison. They did that a lot.

Nicky suddenly became aware of a boy, about her age, standing in front of her in the garden.

''What's the big idea of kissing me five years early?'' he said.

''Huh?'' Nicky answered. Our princess was dumbfounded.

''You kissed me five years too early, stupid,'' the boy answered. ''You were supposed to wait until we were both sixteen. We can't run away together now.''

''Yuck,'' Nicole answered. ''I wouldn't *want* to run away with you!''

The situation didn't look good. Nicky's parents were screaming ''don'ts'' from the deck.

''Don't get your feet wet. Don't ruin your new dress. Don't play with any of those slimy frogs.''

''Slimy, my eye,'' the boy said. ''How would they like to have to catch mosquitoes for a living?''

Nicole turned away. She was starting to get a little sick of his constant complaining.

''But say.'' The boy was coming closer to Ni-cole. ''You've got to kiss me again.''

''Forget it!''

''But if you don't, I'll turn back into a frog!''

''What's it to me?'' Nicole was completely unmoved by his plight.

The boy was already changing. His hands were becoming webbed, and his face was turning green. He was already noticeably shorter.

''Quick!'' he pleaded. ''Hurry! It doesn't have to be a smoochy kiss. One on my forehead would be enough!''

Nicole didn't care. She thought that his forehead was beginning to look rather disgust-ing. And, she thought that the boy would be pretty pesky to have around. Besides, he'd called her stupid.

The boy-frog was getting shorter and shorter and greener and greener. He seemed to finally realize that Nicky wasn't going to help him, and he gave a little gulp and jumped toward the pond. A strange expression came over his frog-boy face, and he turned to Nicky and said, ''Say, I forgot. There *is* one thing I can do.''

''What?'' Nicole was only mildly interested. She was hoping he'd get this turning into a frog business over with. She was starting to get a little bored.

''I can change the name of this place from

the Land of Don't to the Land of Do.''

''You can?'' Nicky's heart started racing.

''I can.'' He kept jumping closer and closer to the pond. ''And I will! In appreciation for all that you've done for me. In appreciation for the future years in which I'm going to have to eat bugs and sleep in slime!'' He made a final jump onto the nearest lily pad, and with his last boy breath, he turned and proclaimed, ''I now pronounce this place THE LAND OF DO!''

Our princess felt a little nervous about the eating bugs and slime part, but she decided to forget about that and concentrate on the good stuff. Royal as she was, our princess was not all that bright.

Thinking about living in the Land of Do, she experienced a moment of pure bliss. No more don'ts, she thought. No more don't do this and don't do that. This is going to be great! Maybe that frog wasn't so bad, after all.

But then, into Nicole's joyous state came a noise, a familiar noise, one that Nicky had heard many times before. It was her parents, once again shouting in chorus from the deck.

''Come in here and do your homework!''

''What?'' said Nicole. ''This doesn't compute!''

''Get in this house this instant and do the dishes. You've left this place a mess!''

Nicole was starting to understand what had

happened. She felt her arms starting to shake.

''Do the vacuuming!'' Their voices were becoming higher and louder. Nicole could tell that they were working themselves into a frenzy of Dos.

''I'll get that stupid frog,'' Nicole yelled, rage in her heart, as she plunged into the pond, grabbing for lily pads, right and left. Frogs were jumping hysterically, frantically trying to keep away from her.

''You're getting mud on your dress,'' her parents shouted. ''Now you're going to have to do the laundry!''

''I'll get him for this!'' Nicky kept screaming, as she plunged in deeper and deeper still.

And, even today, five months later, Nicole can still be seen in the pond of the garden in the Land of Do, which is not very far from here. When asked, she says that she's searching for a skinny, almost emaciated, yellowish looking frog.

Who knows. Maybe someday, she'll find him.

Chapter Twenty

My dear Cassie,

I love your story. I've been reading it and rereading it all week. I love the part where the frog puts Nicole in the Land of Do. She deserves it.

This has been a horrible day. Rob actually called me aside at the beginning of lab, and told me that I didn't have to stay.

"How come?" I asked naively.

"Well, uh," he said, starting to sweat on his forehead. "We're working with the Bunsen burners, and you remember what happened the last time . . ."

"You mean when I purposely tried to burn down the lab?" I asked, smiling sweetly.

"Well, uh, I know you don't mean to, uh, but, uh . . ."

"So, how are you going to justify giving me a B today?" I asked, and I must admit that my voice was raised. People were starting to look.

"Shhhh," he said.

"You started it," I answered.

Sweat was pouring off his forehead. He took a deep breath and said, "Ms. Hannely, do you honestly want me to believe that you actually want to take part in this experiment?"

He had me on that one. "Well, I . . ."

"Do you desire to torment me and everyone else in here with the possibility of injury to our beings? Not to mention, finally and completely, destroying our laboratory?"

That last part was mean, really mean, Cassie. Do you remember when I broke our best salad bowl, back in our apartment? You said, you were only seven then, you said, "Mom, don't cry. You're much more important than that stupid salad bowl."

Cassie put the letter down for a moment, suddenly remembering Aunt Emily's blue glass plate that she'd broken before their party. It seemed like so long ago. Cassie picked up the letter again.

You were smarter than him, Cassie, even at seven. And you certainly were kinder. I mean, I know I'm a klutz. You know I'm a klutz. Anybody who's been around me for more than a couple of hours knows I'm a klutz. It's not like I planned it that way.

And, besides, I never asked to take this stupid chemistry course. It's a stupid requirement.

I've got to go — time to make supper for Mrs. Schneider. She seems okay.

Love and hugs,
Mom

It started out as an ordinary trip to school that Wednesday morning. They'd gotten to Mrs. Parnelli's and Mr. G had stopped the bus and honked twice, like he always did. But Mrs. Parnelli didn't come out.

Mr. G honked again, and then he started getting out of his seat, but then he changed his mind and honked again. Everybody got real quiet on the school bus.

All of a sudden, Mr. G rushed out of his seat and actually ran to Mrs. Parnelli's door. It was locked, so then he banged a few times, and then he did a shocking thing. He picked up one the chairs on the porch and smashed the kitchen window in.

"Wow," Cora said, "Mrs. Parnelli's sure going to be mad at him."

"Shut up, Cora," Anthony said, and Cassie was glad he had. She was starting to feel afraid.

Once Mr. G had smashed all the glass out with the chair legs, he climbed through, his plaid flannel shirt flying out in back. He was inside for only a minute, and then came back, running out the front door.

"Listen kids," he said, "I'm going for help. Anthony, you and . . . you and Cassie go in and stay with her."

"But, what . . ."

"Mrs. Parnelli has fallen down and hurt herself. I'm going to call an ambulance down at Landerson's, and I want you to stay with her until we get back."

Cassie couldn't believe Mr. G had chosen *her*. She was still a little afraid of Mrs. Parnelli, and she didn't like hospital stuff at all. She'd never wanted to be a doctor. But all the kids were quiet, even Cora, and Cassie found herself getting out of her seat and walking down the bus steps and toward the front door with Anthony. Mr. G was already driving off.

"How come he didn't call from here?" she asked Anthony.

"She doesn't have a phone. You know how she hates modern appliances."

Cassie hadn't known, but she kept walking toward the house with Anthony. She wanted to stop, but she didn't want him to know she was afraid.

They got to the door, and Anthony blurted out, "What if she's all bloody or something?"

"I don't know." Cassie grabbed the door handle. She didn't want to go in, but Mr. G was counting on them, and she pushed open the door and walked into the kitchen. Mrs. Parnelli was on the floor, next to the stove. Cassie didn't see any blood, but she did see piles of broken glass on the floor near the refrigerator.

"Come over, dears," Mrs. Parnelli said in a little voice. "I don't bite."

They walked over slowly, and Cassie remembered that she'd seen this TV show once where they'd said never to move an injured person, but to put a blanket over them, if you could. "Do you want me to get you a blanket?" she asked.

"I'd like that. Oh, you . . . you're the skinny one. The skinny new one."

"I've been here almost four months."

"Four months," Mrs. Parnelli repeated softly. Her voice trailed off, and Cassie went into the living room to look for a blanket. She found a red-and-yellow afghan on an old couch in front of the wood stove. As she looked around, she saw glass bottles on every windowsill. Old medicine bottles, Cassie thought. Every bottle sparkled. Every one seemed to have its special place.

"Here," she said, coming back into the kitchen and covering up Mrs. Parnelli. Somehow, it was getting easier to be nice to her. Cassie didn't even mind almost touching her, even though she'd never been this close to an injured person before. "Do you want a pillow?"

"Get the old one in the bedroom," Mrs. Parnelli answered. "The one with the holey top. I don't want to bleed on my new one."

Cassie noticed then that there *was* blood on her forehead. She must have hit it on the side of the stove while she was falling.

The bedroom was neat and clean, with pots of African violets growing on a wicker table by the window. There were purple violets and white ones, and every pot had a ribbon tied around its rim. The ribbons were different colors so that, when Cassie looked quickly at the table, it looked like a garden in full bloom.

The house was so rundown on the outside that Cassie had always thought it would be messy inside. And dirty.

"When did you fall down?" Anthony was asking, when she got back into the kitchen.

"Early this morning, getting my breakfast. I don't know what I would have done if you, if Mr. G hadn't . . ." Her voice broke.

Cassie was shocked to hear her call Mr. Gagnon, Mr. G. She thought that only the kids called him that.

"But," Mrs. Parnelli was talking again. "I'll not think of that. The good Lord was with me today and sent Mr. G and you two to help."

Cassie suddenly felt embarrassed. She was only there because of Mr. G. She wouldn't have come on her own.

Anthony must have been embarrassed, too, because he coughed. Cassie had never heard Anthony cough.

"Does it hurt a lot?" he asked.

"It hurts," Mrs. Parnelli answered. She moved her right arm to fix the blanket and, as she did, her hand brushed against a locket on the floor. "Oh, it fell off. It broke." For the first time, she looked like she was going to cry.

Cassie stooped and picked up the locket to hand it to her. "Here."

"Oh, no, it could get lost in the hospital. The chain must have broken as I fell. I think . . . I think I remember grabbing for it."

"Please don't cry. I'll take care of it for you."

"Will you? Will you be a dear and do that for me? I'd feel so much better . . ." She looked away.

Anthony and Cassie sat down on the kitchen floor near her, brushing away stray glass from the broken window. They sat, looking away from each other, suddenly not knowing what to say.

Mrs. Parnelli closed her eyes and settled her head into the pillow. After a few minutes, Cassie thought that maybe she was asleep. But then, she became afraid that maybe she'd stopped breathing. Cassie looked at Mrs. Parnelli more closely and saw her mouth moving slightly, in tiny motions, as though she was talking to herself.

Cassie put her hand in her jacket pocket and felt the locket. It was still there. Then, she put the locket in her inside pocket, the one that had the zipper, to make sure it wouldn't get lost.

They finally heard the ambulance coming up the hill. The sounds seemed to upset Mrs. Parnelli.

"Don't let them take me," she said, trying to reach for Cassie's hand.

"What?"

"Don't let them . . ."

All of a sudden, a man and a woman were rushing in the door and stooping down next to Mrs. Parnelli, taking her blood pressure and listening to her heart. Mr. G was standing in the doorway.

"Okay, Pete," the woman said, "let's go."

Just like that, they had Mrs. Parnelli on a stretcher and were taking her out the door. She grabbed for Mr. G's hand as she went by, and he reached for her.

"Stop for a second," he said to Pete and the woman.

"Don't let them take me," Mrs. Parnelli said.

"It's okay, it's okay. You need help. You have to go. But I promise you, Mrs. Parnelli, I will personally bring you home when you're well."

"You'll bring me home? You promise?"

"I promise."

"You two did a great job," Mr. G said, as they walked toward the bus.

"How come she got like that? I thought she *wanted* to go to the hospital?" Cassie asked.

"She knows she has to, but she's afraid. She's afraid she'll never be able to come home."

"What's the matter with her? Will she be okay?"

"She may have broken her hip."

"How come she wants to live here so much?"

"It's her home. She wants to be home."

Just like me, Cassie thought. She wants to be home, just like me.

Somehow, though, Cassie was becoming confused about where home was. Was it in South Braintree with her mom, living in a little apartment with Mom working all the time, with lots of noise and not being able to go out alone at night? Or was it in this funny half-farmland, half-mountain place, with snakes and cows and trees and ponds and a kid who lied about his age and a school where they let her write funny stories? If only Mom were here, she could tell her where home was. If only Mom were here . . .

They were only half an hour late getting to school, so nobody could understand why Mrs. Blanchette was so mad. She met the bus as soon as it stopped, and didn't bother to wait until the kids got off before she started yelling at Mr. G.

"Where *were* you? What is the meaning of this? I will not have you cavorting around the neighborhood, endangering these children's lives. I will not have you running around the neighborhood . . ." She stopped. It seemed like she was searching for the proper words to list the awful crimes Mr. G had committed. Putting both hands on her head, she actually started pulling on her strawberry blonde hair. She took a deep breath and went on. "You are the most . . . the most irresponsible person I have ever had working for me, and furthermore — "

Mr. G stood up and faced her. "In the first place, Mrs. Blanchette, I was not cavorting around the neighborhood." Even though he was shorter than Mrs. Blanchette, he appeared to be growing taller. His voice seemed to rise in the air until, finally, it, too, was speaking down to her. "And in the second place, I would never, under any circumstances, endanger these children. And, furthermore, I do not work for you, I work for them." His arm swung back toward the bus. Every person was somehow included, and Cassie breathed a deep sigh. "Now, will you please get off the steps of my bus and let them get to class. They are already late."

Mrs. Blanchette released her hair and let her arms fall by her side. She turned and walked off the bus and back into the building, without ever looking back.

Mr. G sighed and said, quite calmly, "Okay, everybody, get to class."

Class meeting was over by the time Cassie and Cora and Anthony got to class.

"Oh, I'm glad you're all here," Mrs. Kalish said, "I didn't think you *all* could be absent."

"Mrs. Parnelli's gonna die," Cora said. "Mr. G found her, and . . ."

"She's not going to *die*," Cassie heard herself saying. "She just broke her hip or something."

"Cassie and I stayed with her while Mr. G got the ambulance."

"And Mrs. Blanchette yelled at Mr. G and . . ."

Suddenly everybody was talking at once.

"Weren't you scared?"

"What did she yell at him for?"

"Was Mrs. Parnelli crying?"

Even Mrs. Kalish was talking. "Is she going to be okay?"

Mrs. Kalish actually let them stop reading and talk about it for ten minutes. Then they had to get back to work.

At recess, Laura came over and asked Cassie if she wanted to play Four Square, and Bethany asked her to play Giant Checkers. Sarah told her she was saving her a swing. That Wednesday, the recess bell rang too soon.

Chapter Twenty-one

Dear Cassie,

Well, she's finally done it this time. I was in Mrs. Schneider's room getting her laundry when I just happened to check her closet to see if any dirty clothes had fallen on the floor.

There was a dirty sock, and when I bent down to pick it up, I saw the box. It was a cardboard box, big, at least two-and-a-half feet across, and I was sure I'd never seen it before.

That's where she slipped. She forgot to close the top. If it had been closed, I never would have looked inside. I would have wanted to, but I'd never invade her privacy. A closed box is a closed box.

But it was open, and when I looked in, there they were: candy bars, layer after layer of candy bars! There were 3 Musketeers and Snickers and Almond Joys, and every kind of candy bar you could imagine!

Naturally, I called Merilyn, and she came right over and got to the bottom of it. Mrs. Schneider has sold the furniture she's been storing in the attic! She called some dealer, and he came over when I was at school and, according to Mrs. Schneider, gave her a darn good price. Mrs. Schneider said that now she could afford years of candy bars.

Merilyn had a fit. Mrs. Schneider said that it was her furniture, and she could darn well do what she wanted with it. She said it was her body, too, and if she wanted to eat junk food, we should darn well keep our noses out of her business. When Merilyn and I had lived long and active lives like she had, then *we* had the right to tell her what to do.

Merilyn started crying and telling her she loved her, and Mrs. Schneider said that a lot of injustice could be done in the name of love, and why didn't we stay out of her life?

The funny thing is, Cassie, that I think she has a point. I mean, maybe if we let her eat the junk food, maybe she wouldn't want to so much after a while. But it *is* her right to decide.

Oh, and Rob called. He said that he didn't mean to make me cry, and he'd let me come back to the lab if I wanted to.

We're going to the movies Friday night. He's just a kid, but it'll be fun to do something different, with a friend.

Must run. I gotta start studying for finals.

Love,
Mom

Dear Mom,

Mrs. Parnelli, the lady we get groceries for every Wednesday on schooltime, almost died. She was all bloody and stuff and Mr. G made Anthony and me stay with her.

Mrs. Blanchette and Mr. G had a big fight, right in front of us, and . . .

It wasn't true. It was a little true, but the way she was telling it was a lie. Cassie tore the letter into a thousand pieces and threw it in the trash.

Cassie wanted to give the locket back to Mrs. Parnelli. Mr. G had said that she'd be in the hospital for a couple of weeks, at least, and then she'd probably go to a nursing home until she could manage at home by herself. He said that some of the neighbors were already arranging a schedule to stop by a few times a day to help her with the wood stove, until the winter was over.

"Look, it's got a picture in it," Cassie said, handing the locket to Aunt Emily as they were having breakfast together.

"It's beautiful." She picked up the locket and examined the tiny picture that you could see when you opened the clasp.

"But who are they?"

"It may be Mrs. Parnelli and her husband on their wedding day."

"But she's so pretty. And Mrs. Parnelli's *old*. She doesn't look like that at all."

Aunt Emily laughed. "That's called aging, my dear, it happens to the best of us."

"Do you think she'll like that it's fixed?"

"She'll love it. It was a great idea to ask Ernie's father to fix it."

"Ernie helped."

"He did?"

"He knows how to do all that stuff." Cassie picked up the locket again, and examined it more closely. "Maybe I could mail it to her, but . . . she *did* ask me to keep it for her. Do you think I could bring it to her at the hospital?"

"I wonder if they'd let you?" Aunt Emily asked, looking up from her coffee. "I'll call. I'll see if they'll let us come."

"Us?"

"Well, I'll go with you in case they won't let you in without a grown-up. Do you mind?"

"No, I mean, I'm glad you'll come."

Aunt Emily called the hospital, and the nurse said that Mrs. Parnelli could have visitors.

"Can we go now?" Cassie asked.

"Give me about half an hour to shower and get dressed, and then I'll be ready."

It smelled like a hospital. The only other time Cassie had ever been in a hospital was when her mom had her wisdom teeth removed, and they'd kept her overnight. Cassie had been scared then, too.

The white-haired lady at the desk told them that Mrs. Parnelli was in C-45, that they had to follow the yellow line on the floor to her room. They kept walking down corridor after corridor, some lined with paintings, others defined by glass walls with open courtyards on either side. Cassie figured that there was nobody in the hospital, that there were only empty halls.

They finally got to some double doors that said Rooms C-30 to C-75. When they found Mrs. Parnelli's room, Cassie thought at first that nobody was there, that maybe the lady at the desk had given them the wrong room. But then she saw her, lying in the bed closest to the window. She was lying completely still.

Mrs. Parnelli didn't seem to notice that they were there. She was just lying in bed, straight on her back, staring at the ceiling. Aunt Emily walked over to her, to the side of the bed, and put her hands on the railings. Cassie followed behind and stood next to Aunt Emily.

"Mrs. Parnelli."

"Oh, Emily. Oh, and this is your daughter." Mrs. Parnelli smiled at Cassie.

"She's my niece. But, I hope we're not disturbing you."

"Oh, no, I'm just resting."

"Cassie has something for you."

Cassie pulled the locket out of her pocket and put it in Mrs. Parnelli's open hand. "I got it fixed for you," she said.

Mrs. Parnelli seemed surprised by the gift. She closed her fingers around the locket and slowly drew it toward her. She opened her hand again, and then examined the locket closely, not saying anything, just turning it over and over. "My husband gave this to me," she said, "when we were married."

"Do you want me to still keep it for you?" Cassie asked, "I mean, in case you're afraid it will get lost in here?"

Mrs. Parnelli pulled the locket close to her.

"Oh, no. You fixed it?"

"Ernie and his father did."

Mrs. Parnelli clutched the locket even more tightly, then suddenly turned pale, very pale. Cassie got scared that she'd made the wrong decision to bring the locket to her. But Aunt Emily just moved closer to Mrs. Parnelli and said, "Do you want me to put it on for you?"

"Please, yes, I'd be so grateful. I've missed it. It would comfort me so much."

Aunt Emily put the locket around Mrs. Parnelli's neck, and Cassie was *so* glad that she'd come with her. Somehow, Aunt Emily knew what to do.

"Maybe you'll come visit me when I get home," Mrs. Parnelli said.

"We'd love to do that."

"I'll make you oatmeal raisin cookies."

Aunt Emily laughed. "Now, how do you remember that those are my favorite?"

"The last time you were over to help with the wood, you ate five of them."

"Five?" Cassie asked. Mrs. Parnelli's cookies were huge. Of course, Aunt Emily did have quite a reputation for her cookie consumption.

The sunlight was coming through the window now. It made Cassie remember the tiny bottles in Mrs. Parnelli's windows, in her living room.

"What about your African violets?" she asked.

"Oh, Mr. G is taking care of them."

Cassie felt glad. Mrs. Parnelli settled back into her pillow, and it seemed like the time to leave.

"Thank you so much," Mrs. Parnelli said to Cassie, taking her hand. "You don't know how much this means to me." She looked at Aunt Emily. "Thank you for coming. You have a lovely daughter."

"Thank you." That was all that Aunt Emily said.

In the car, Cassie asked her about it. "How come she keeps thinking you're my mother?"

"She's sick. She probably has a fever. She'll be okay in time."

"Will she really be able to go home?"

"I think so. She'll need help from the neighbors and Visiting Nurse care and some social work help, but . . . you know, that's the kind of work your mom wants to do when she graduates."

"How come?"

"How come what?"

"How come she wants to do that?"

"I don't know. I guess I've thought that your mom and I both like older people because our parents died so young. And we both loved them so much."

"Oh." Cassie sat, staring out the window. "Aunt Emily?"

"Yes, dear?"

"Even if I don't live here anymore, will you bring me to see Mrs. Parnelli?"

"Yes, I will."

"And . . . and can I spend weekends and stuff with you and Uncle Fred?"

"But, Cassie, you're going to be with us another five months."

"I know, but . . . if I have to go back to Boston . . ."

"You know what? I don't want you worrying about this. If your mom gets a job in Boston, Uncle Fred and I will come pick you up and bring you back here for visits."

"Really?"

"I wouldn't have it any other way."

For the rest of the way home, they were quiet. Cassie didn't even feel like putting on the radio. They rode in silence, Aunt Emily driving along without her usual comments, and Cassie looking out the window. When they turned off exit 34 and were driving up the ramp, Aunt Emily said, "You know, I wouldn't mind being your mother."

"You wouldn't?"

"No, I'd like it."

"Oh."

"I'm proud of you."

"You are?"

"Yes."

"Why?"

"Because you're smart and good, and you did a really wonderful thing for Mrs. Parnelli."

"I only brought back her locket."

"You gave her a lot more than that."

"Oh." Cassie felt embarrassed, so she put on the radio.

When they got back into town, they got ice cream at the creamery. Aunt Emily got a medium because she was still on a diet, and Cassie got a large chocolate with butterscotch dip. Then they went home and finished off the last of the ginger snaps.

Chapter Twenty-two

Dear Mom,

Okay, now look. I like it here better than I used to, but it's still not fair.

You shouldn't've dumped me off like that, on a Sunday. We should've come up together during the summer and spent a couple of weeks, so I could've gotten used to it with you here. We could've at least spent a week here together, instead of us just staying home when you had vacation.

And you should've told me you were leaving as soon as you knew. You should have told me even when you were thinking about it. We should've talked about it. You shouldn't've just told me.

How do you think I felt, just dumped off like that?

And it wasn't a very nice thing to do to Aunt Emily and Uncle Fred, either, you know. I mean, I was a pain to them. It wasn't fair to them at all. Or to me. I was really mad at you.

Now this thing about Mrs. Parnelli. Aunt Emily's been gushing about how great I was, but all I did was go in with Anthony because Mr. G told us to, and I couldn't get out of it. I wouldn't've gone in on my own. And she's a nice lady. That's why I asked Ernie to fix her locket.

And I'm not happy at all about this Christmas thing. But Cora and me are gonna start a baby-sitting business. We're gonna advertise and be a team. That way we don't have to do it alone in some of the places that are so far out.

Is that okay with you? Aunt Emily and Uncle Fred say that I'm old enough, especially if I do it with Cora.

Anyway, with the tons of money I make baby-sitting, I'm going to call you on Christmas. And we can talk as long as we like. We don't even have to use the timer.

Cora's mother says that a rural environment is better than an urban environment in which to raise a child. I think she's right. How about we live here when you get out of school?

I gotta go. Ernie and me are gonna go skating on the pond. Don't worry, it's frozen solid. Mr. Brennar was on there with his truck yesterday, plowing off the snow.

I miss you tons and tons. Aunt Emily's

gonna buy me a special calendar and we're gonna mark off the weeks till you come home.

Your daughter,
Cassie

About the Author

Cynthia Stowe made her publishing debut with *Home Sweet Home, Good-Bye* for Scholastic Hardcover. *Dear Mom, in Ohio for a Year* is her second book. Ms. Stowe has worked with children for many years. She especially enjoys teaching them writing.

A native of New Britain, Connecticut, Ms. Stowe currently lives with her husband, Robert, in western Massachusetts.